GENERATION IMPACT:
AN AMERICAN FAMILY'S TURMOIL

VIRANDA I. SLAPPY

STONEWALL PRESS

PAVING YOUR WAY TO SUCCESS

Library of Congress Control Number: 2017958492
eBook: 978-1-948172-02-8
Softcover: 978-1-948172-03-5
Hardcover: 978-1-948172-14-1

STONEWALL PRESS
PAVING YOUR WAY TO SUCCESS

Stonewall Press
363 Paladium Court
Owings Mills, MD 21117
www.stonewallpress.com
1-888-334-0980

It gives me great pleasure to dedicate this book to Willie Mae Purnell.
You will never be forgotten, and you will be loved always.

ACKNOWLEDGMENT

First, I give honor to God for bestowing me the talent to create this story.

I extend special thanks to all the people who helped make it possible for this reality-based book to be available for all to read.

To my husband and children, thanks for the loving support and time you allowed for me to write this story.

To my grandmother, thank you for your love, knowledge, wisdom, and faith. As my role model, you inspired the development of the skills I needed to produce this book.

To my relatives and friends, thanks for your love and support.

To my editors, Beth Mansbridge, Andrew Hamilton, and Zsashamica D. Slappy, thanks for the patience, knowledge, skills, and ability that you bestowed to produce this book.

To my book artist, Patrick St. Clair, thanks for your artistic talents in creating my book cover.

To my readers, you are my inspiration. Thanks for devoting your time and enthusiasm, and for the purchase of all my books.

INTRODUCTION

This story is based on the legacy of an African-American family's journey from the mid-1940s through the early '90s. The struggles faced by this family include child abuse, drugs, teenage pregnancy, gang violence, and more. This saga is revealed to you through a family that strives to succeed despite its setbacks. *Generation Impact* reveals the mental anguish and the triumphs of the Turner family (Thomas and Willie Mae) and their descendants.

Contents

MID-FORTIES

Stopping just outside of Lee's Grocery Store, Mrs. Sara Lee checked her watch after she spotted Willie Mae's son, Bro Turner, and a friend loitering on the street corner when they should have been in school. She immediately called out to Bro.

Frankie said, "Hey, Bro, did you hear Mrs. Sara Lee calling you?"

"No."

The neighborhood "policewoman" waved at them and called his name again.

Frankie poked Bro's arm. "Well, do you hear her now?"

"Yap, I hear her. She done seen me now. She is going to tell mom that I played hooky again. Man, I hate going to school! I want to get me a job making a lot of money so I can help my mama."

"Don't your policeman daddy make no money?" Frankie asked.

Out of the corners of their eyes, the teenagers watched Mrs. Sara Lee as she waited to cross the street.

"Yap, but he don't give my mama any money. He takes his money and do what he want to do with it. My mama be tired every night when she come home from working at that laundry plant. My sister Dot sees after my sisters, brother, and me. My daddy doesn't help my mama do anything. He too busy walkin' the beat with that big black stick in his hand. He got in trouble one time 'cause he arrested this white man. He knew that he wasn't supposed to arrest the white men, but he wanted to be the big man. I overheard my mama and him fussing about him letting his job go to his head," Bro blabbed.

Mrs. Sara Lee, walking slowly because of her lame left leg approached, saying, "Bro, I see you boys. Y'all didn't go to school today. I'm going to tell Willie."

She stood there waiting a few moments while the boys looked down at the sidewalk, watching her right foot tapping—tapping.

"Humph!" she said and wobbled away, grocery bag swinging against her cane.

Frankie complained. "Man, that lady is nosey! You can't do anything without Mrs. Sara Lee not knowing about it. I better be going. See you later," he said with a wave of his hand and broke into a run.

Bro was not aware that Dot had gotten ill at school and had gone home early. Hearing the door being unlocked, Dot got up from her bed and found her brother getting a drink of water in the kitchen.

"Daddy going to beat your butt, Bro. You should have gone to school. I don't know why you don't want to go to that school," said Dot.

Bro brushed past Dot without a comment and went out the front door.

True to her word, Mrs. Sara Lee came over that evening, revealing her secret to Willie. Later, Willie Mae's discipline was a whipping on Bro's backside with a belt. She threatened to tell his father. But she never really intended on telling Thomas, hoping that Bro would mend his ways.

Mrs. Sara Lee ran into Sergeant Turner at the grocery store at lunch time the next day. "Thomas, I can see you are working… but one quick word. I just want to check to see how Bro is getting along. He's a nice young man. I don't know why he don't like going to school. You and Willie Mae does all y'all can to raise those children up right."

Thomas wanted to interrupt her right then but knew that Mrs. Sara Lee would talk nonstop till she had said her piece, so he didn't.

She continued, "Bro sure loves hanging around Carlton and his boys, building homes. But like I told Willie Mae, he needs to go to school first, get him a degree, so that he can get his own business to build homes."

Thomas was surprised. He wasn't aware that Bro was missing school. He thanked Mrs. Sara Lee and rushed out of the grocery store. He sped to the school to check to see whether Bro was there. The teacher told him she hadn't seen Bro in a couple of weeks.

Thomas went home to wait for his wife. As soon as she came home from work, he demanded to know what she knew about it. They argued and he burst out the door to go look for Bro. Willie Mae was scared. She had never seen Thomas so angry. Dot had heard it all through the thin walls. "Mama, Bro is in big trouble."

Willie told Dot to hold off going to get the other kids from her grandmother's, and to get back to her bedroom. Willie Mae prayed aloud, "Lord, I hope that boy comes home first before Thomas finds him."

Her prayers went silent as she pictured in her mind back in the mid- '40s. Thomas Turner, a young and handsome colored man marring Willie Mae, a fifteen-year-old, light-brownish colored girl. Marriage among young teenagers was common then. Over their thirty-nine years of marriage, Thomas and Willie had seven children. As a typical couple, the husband headed the household and worked while the wife stayed home and raised the children.

Thomas was from Montgomery, Alabama. He was charming and was very popular with the women. Willie Mae Browning, also from Alabama, was an only child. She matured into a strong, quiet, friendly woman who showed more patience for her husband's goings-on than he deserved. She was close to her mother, Frannie Mae Browning, an American Indian- mixed colored with long, straight black hair, who lived down the street and provided much-needed constant moral support and babysitting services.

As Willie Mae reminisced and prayed, Thomas checked out the area where Mr. Carlton was building new homes. There he spotted Bro. He waited a block away until Mr. Carlton and the rest of the men left for the day. Bro gathered his belongings and began walking home. Glancing up from the ground, he noticed a police car coming in his direction. Fearing that it could be his dad, he ran into the thick woods and hid among the bushes, watching until the police car cruised by. When the street was deserted, he continued walking along until the police car pulled up from behind—he was trapped.

It *was* his dad. Yelling from the car window, Thomas commanded, "Get in, boy! Where do you think you are going?"

"Dad, I'm coming from school. I promised the teacher that I would help her grade some papers."

"Boy, you are lying. But you will learn not to lie to me no more. Now, get in."

Bro reluctantly slipped onto the front seat of the cruiser for the deathly-silent ride home.

That evening after work, Thomas Turner took Bro to an abandoned house and beat him with his black stick. He beat him bad. He then drove Bro home, ordered him out of the car in front of their house, and left. Bro could barely walk. Dot, seeing her brother, screamed out for her mama, ran outside to grab her brother, who collapsed in her arms.

Willie rushed out of the house to their side. She searched her boy's face. His eyes were swollen shut.

"Lord! Boy, who did this to you? Where have you been?"

"Mom, daddy beat me," Bro whispered, clinging to his mama's dress. "Dot, go quick and get Mrs. Sara Lee, she knows what to do." Willie sopped up the streaming facial blood with her clean apron. "Hang on, Bro. Dot gone to get help. Lord… Thomas will pay for this!"

Dot and Willie Mae helped a groaning Bro to his bedroom. Mrs. Sara Lee and Willie Mae treated Bro's broken skin wounds and, though it obviously pained him, tested him for broken bones. They sat vigil in Bro's room.

Mrs. Sara Lee confessed that it was her fault. "I saw Thomas earlier today at the market and I told him about Bro not going to school."

"Don't you go blaming yourself, Mrs. Sara Lee," Willie said, patting her friend's hands. "Thomas done wearin' the big head ever since he got that job at the police station. But he had gone too far this time. He isn't going to beat my child like this. No, he isn't going to beat my child no more. I'll see to that."

"Willie, what are you going to do?"

"I'm going down to that police station and tell them what he did to his own child. They can come back with me and see for themselves. No, a man has no business being a policeman, beating their own child like this. I don't care what Bro did, he didn't have to beat him. Will you stay and watch Bro till I get back?" asked Willie.

"Take as much time as you need," Mrs. Sara Lee replied.

Willie Mae went to the police station and officially reported the incident. Thomas was considered an outstanding officer in the department. One would never think that he would lose control and beat his own child. His colleagues were very disappointed, embracing and comforting Willie Mae as she continued to tell her story.

An investigation was conducted but no trial was held due to the distraught demeanor of the family. Bro refused to testify against his father at all, blaming himself for his father's failure. Willie Mae felt guilty about her decision to expose the family crisis to the police. After a two-week investigation, Thomas Turner was kicked off the police force.

Bro soon joined the army. A year later, Dot went to college. Six months later, Thomas found a job in the produce department at the local market.

DOUBLE VISION

The army assigned Bro to Korea. He wrote to his mother and sent money to help the family out. Willie Mae thought it better not to tell her husband about Bro's money. She used it to help Dot with her college fees. Willie Mae missed not having her older children at home, but she knew they were trying to make something out of themselves.

Bertha and Martha, identical twins, were very pretty. Guys couldn't stay away from the girls; consequently, their parents were very protective of them. At sixteen, they were next in the pecking order to help Willie Mae care for the three younger children while she worked. Bertha was especially sensitive to the way their father treated their mother. She was aware he never gave her any money, and all he did was buy some food and pay a few of their bills.

Willie Mae didn't hear from her son for much of 1949. She began to worry that something might have happened to him. She talked with her supervisor at work who told her to contact the Red Cross if she didn't hear from him soon.

Thomas drifted in and out of their lives, apparently not concerned about Bro. Months passed with Willie Mae and the children just barely surviving. Her mother, Frannie Mae, helped with the youngest children while Bertha and Martha went to work in the fields to harvest vegetables and pick cotton.

One hot afternoon in the cotton fields, the girls sat under a lone oak tree, having a discussion about their future. Martha wiped her forehead with an already damp handkerchief.

"We got to help mama out," Martha said. "I read in the newspaper about women joining the Air Force. I'm going to join the Air Force. We've got to do something more to help."

"The Air Force," Bertha repeated. She halted the inspection of her rough palms and gazed over her sister's shoulder. "It sounds like it would beat working out here in these fields. Can you imagine seeing yourself in those uniforms? We'd sure make mom and dad proud of us."

"I don't know about dad but I do know that mom would be. She hasn't heard from Bro in months. I know that's what's been on her mind lately. I pray that he's alright."

"I pray for him too."

Bro had sustained a severe head injury during combat and was hospitalized at the Army Base Medical Battalion in Seoul. One night while in the hospital, Bro had a dream about his ordeal. His vision revealed him trapped in a foxhole with Private Scott, a soldier who had sustained injury on his left shoulder. They were holed up in jungle fields, 164 miles outside of Osan, Korea. During a long twilight, they crouched and listened to the intermittent explosion of shells but could not detect the source of fire. After fifteen minutes of silence, Bro tapped his watch with his finger and gave a thumbs-up. Scott nodded. They hoped they had a break. Bro gently grabbed Scott's arm, checking to see how severe the injury was. Bro whispered, "Damn, man, you sure are lucky! I think you're going to make it. Now, I got to figure out how I'm going to get you to the vehicle." He ripped Scott's sleeve and made a bandage for his shoulder. "OK. I think this will hold until I get you to the dispensary." Bro placed Scott's right arm around his neck, raised Scott up slowly, and peered at the landscape. All clear. It was a struggle to climb out. Together, they stumbled through the jungle as quickly as possible, heading for the jeep. When they were only a few yards away, firing sounded off and Bro's head was hit.

In shock, Bro woke up from his dream, screaming for Scott. The night duty nurse rushed into his room, trying to calm Bro down and calling another nurse to get the doctor.

Bro threw off the bed covers and looked around, ready to jump out of bed. "I don't need a doctor. What happened to my soldier, Private Scott?"

"Private Scott?" the nurse asked.

Scott was just then arriving for his nightly visit. He strode to the bedside and held Bro by the shoulders. "Corporal Turner, calm down now. Hey, I'm fine… no, *we* are OK, man. Thanks to you," Private Scott said.

Two weeks later, Bro recovered enough to be thrown back into the Korean War.

Bro finally returned home, safe and unannounced, touching everyone with his homecoming. Thomas embraced his son and welcomed him back. The dutiful son stood at attention and didn't return the sentiments. Bro gave his mother two hundred dollars cash, which she reluctantly accepted, doing so only after Bro insisted.

"Mom, I know you need it." Bro was aware that Thomas was watching from the far end of the living room. Bro bent over to give his mama a long hug and whispered in her ear, "Dad isn't giving you any money. Go buy yourself something pretty."

His mother returned the hug, saying out loud, "You have always worried about me. You don't have to worry, 'cause God is going to work it out."

Thomas strode across the room, snatched the money from Willie Mae's hand, threw it at his son, and left the house. Willie Mae and the other children sat and watched the all-too-familiar scene unfold. Bro didn't say a word. He gathered the money up from the floor and stuffed it in his pocket. He went to his grandmother's house and gave her the two hundred dollars to give to his mother. He explained what happened at home with his dad. His grandmother said that he could live with her. He eagerly accepted her offer.

Martha and Bertha joined the Air Force in 1953. They were the first African-American twins in US Air Force history. It was a dream come true for them compared to the lifestyle they were used to.

They were attractive in their sharp uniforms and the guys went crazy over them. Martha liked to flirt. She never could date only one guy; she preferred a variety. Bertha, always known as "the shy one," couldn't understand her sister's behavior. They both trained as nurses, and arranged for allotments of money to go to their mother every paycheck. The checks were sent to their grandmother's address to circumvent Thomas. They knew that without such an arrangement, their brother and sisters wouldn't get anything despite their mother's best intentions.

Enjoying a relatively peaceful life at his grandmother's, Bro started working with Mr. Carlton as an assistant foreman. Eventually, he felt proficient enough in all aspects of home building and started his own business. Pleased with his newfound prosperity, he started hanging with the fellows in local clubs.

One night, Bro met a foxy young black lady named Christine Matthew. *Boy*, he thought. *Was she fine!* Everything he ever wanted in a lady.

Six months later, Bro said to his mother, "Mom, you know that I've been going with Christine for a while now. I want to ask her to marry me. I want you to know that I'm still going to give you money."

Willie Mae was not surprised at his news. "Bro, if you want to marry this girl, then do so. I don't want you to worry about me. I want you to be happy." She gave her first-born son a long hug, releasing him to a new life.

The next spring, Bro and Christine married. They stayed with her mother while he finished building their own home. He did continue to give his mother financial support.

Stationed in Houston, Texas, Bertha and Martha were living it up. Although Bertha had dated quite a few guys, she still hadn't met anyone worth her serious consideration. One evening, Bertha and Martha went to The Jazz Club. Bertha excused herself from the table and went to the restroom. Watching her from the bar was a handsome young black man. When she returned to the table, the young man approached and asked her for a dance. He smiled as he escorted Bertha to the center of the room. Gently reaching for her hands, he drew her close to his body as they danced to Nat King Cole's hit, "Mona Lisa."

"I couldn't help noticing you and your sister when y'all first walked in. You're identical to your sister."

"Yep, we're twins."

"Very attractive twins at that. But you appear to be the quiet or shy type. Am I wrong in my judgment of you?" he asked.

"No, why would you say that?"

"Your sister came into the club, giggling and flirting. You didn't." He looked into her eyes and raised his eyebrows for half a moment. He smiled.

"Martha has always been like that," answered Bertha. She liked his easy way and smooth dancing.

He asked, "Tell me, are you from here?"

"No, we're in the Air Force. Our home is in Montgomery, Alabama."

"That's where I'm from!"

"Oh, and you're in the Air Force, too?"

"No, I'm in the army, stationed at Fort Hood, Texas. You haven't told me your name—I didn't mean to be impolite—my name is Will Cleveland. What yours?"

"Bertha Turner."

The song ended, and they returned to her table. Bertha introduced Will to Martha and her friends.

"Bertha, he's cute," Martha whispered.

"I know," Bertha replied, smiling. That evening Bertha felt she was finally learning the meaning of *fun*.

Since Will wasn't stationed at Bertha's base, he arranged to see her on weekends. Will and Bertha had been dating for eight months. Fearing that Bertha would marry Will—separating the twins for the first time— Martha had a nervous breakdown.

Bertha contacted their mother and arranged for her to come to Texas. Their mother's visit helped Martha recover. One day, when Bertha left the hospital room to report for duty, Martha revealed to her mother her fear of losing her sister.

Her mother explained that it was only natural for her to have these feelings. "You girls have been close since birth. Y'all are twins, for heaven's sake! I'm sure that Bertha would never think of living too far from you."

"Mom, promise me you won't tell Bertha. She is so happy. Will is so good to her. You got to meet him."

"I've already met him."

"So, isn't he handsome and sweet?"

"Yes he is, but... never mind."

"Never mind what?"

"Nothing," Willie Mae exclaimed. "Tell me, when are you getting out?"

"Tomorrow, I hope. I told them that I wanted to spend time with you before you leave."

Willie Mae enjoyed her visit. She hated to leave, but she had to get back to her family.

Bertha and Martha's time in the service was coming to an end. Will's time was short too. He asked Bertha to marry him. Bertha was reluctant because of their careers, but Will said that he was getting out and wanted to settle down. He had a job as a manager at Warehouse Company waiting for him back home. In her usual cautious manner, Bertha accepted the offer only after she was certain about his future plans.

Six months after Bertha and Will married, Martha married Fred Bradshaw. He was Mrs. Sara Lee's sister's son, also called "Shortman" because of his height. Fred was smart, an honor roll student throughout high school. Bertha had an uneasy feeling that Martha didn't love Fred and assumed Martha got married because she herself was married. She kept her thoughts to herself and wished her twin sister the best.

BETRAYAL

It was April when Bro and Christine finally moved into their new home. Christine was overwhelmed with developing the bare landscape. She busied herself shopping for plants and evergreen scrub for their land. Their home brought joy to all the family as they pitched in to help with the open house family celebration. Willie Mae fell in love with the new house. She spent lots of her time with Christine, helping her decorate.

Thomas, feeling left out, decided to drop by his son's house for a look while Bro was at work. He saw for himself proof of the natural talent for construction that Bro had always shown, even as a child. Occasionally, he would drop by to visit with his son's wife.

After nine months of marriage, Martha and Fred announced Martha's pregnancy. Martha immediately phoned her sister. Surprised and overwhelmed upon hearing the news, Bertha expressed her congratulations.

Henry took overthe duties of being man of the house when Bro left for the service. He was very proud of his older brother's accomplishments, especially since their father was never there much for any of them. Thomas and Henry had a distant father-and-son relationship. Henry was tall for his fifteen years; handsome, bony, and with a light brown complexion. He couldn't stand the sight of his father. Since his childhood, he knew his father didn't give a damn about his mother and was aware of his fucking around with other women.

Henry had witnessed his father fooling around on his mother, although he never told her. On a sunny day, he took the long way home through Fort Hill Cemetery and saw his father across the street on the front porch of a house kissing a woman. He was shocked and angry. Tears blurred the awful scene as he thought, *My mother has worked her butt off in that hot-ass laundry to help support us seven kids who she raised for that selfish womanizer!* That wasn't all that Henry had seen. One day, Henry's grandmother asked him to drop off Bro's clothes that his mama had cleaned for him. As Henry approached his brother's house, he noticed his daddy's car parked out in the yard. He paused, thinking, *What is he doing here? Bro can't be home because I don't see his truck.* Reluctant to enter the area, Henry turned the corner and parked his car a couple blocks away. He found some bushes from where he could watch the door to the house. He prayed the neighbors weren't calling the cops on him.

Minutes later, Thomas came out. Christine waved goodbye and closed the door. Once Henry saw his father's car pull off, he came out from hiding and knocked on the door.

Answering the door while smoothing her hair, Christine exclaimed, "Henry, what brings you over here!"

"Grandma wanted me to bring Bro's clothes over."

"Well, come in. It's got to be hot out there. Your brother isn't here but you're welcome to stay until he comes home. Put those down right there." "No, I can't stay. They'll be worried, since I didn't tell grandma that I w uld be staying." Although the whole family knew about Bro's ban on having Thomas in his house, Henry asked, "Has my daddy been over to see this pretty house?"

"No, I haven't seen your father.... What's the matter? Did I say something wrong?"

He turned toward the door. "No, I got to be going before it gets too dark. Mama starts to worry when the sun goes down. Tell my brother hello." In tears, Henry rushed off, heading for home.

Coming in the back door, he couldn't avoid his sister Irene seeing him. She asked, "Did you take Bro those clothes? Wait a minute… look at me… you've been crying. What are you crying about?"

"Nothing! I hate living here. I hate Dad. I'm going to leave this damn place. I feel sorry for you and Susan."

"Tell me, Henry… what's wrong?"

"You're better off not knowing," was all Henry said before hurrying into his bedroom.

A couple months later, Bertha and Will announced their pregnancy. Soon after, Christine and Bro announced their pregnancy.

One evening, Thomas and Willie Mae were relaxing and talking in front of the fireplace. Willie Mae boasted, "The Lord sure has been good to us. Four of our children are grown and starting families."

"Willie Mae, I guess you're feeling old, 'cause I am not," Thomas commented.

"You may not say that you are an old man, but honey, those 'grands' will say it all," a smiling Willie Mae reminded him.

But it was not wedded bliss all around. Bro and Christine were having marital problems. Christine complained of Bro's working long hours and not spending time with their daughter. Bro argued that he was just trying to make some money to pay for their new home and provide for his family. Christine insisted that as owner of his own business, he could afford to take more time off.

Henry joined the army when he reached his eighteenth birthday. The army assigned him to Germany. He liked the service, especially his job as a military police officer. Two months into his assignment, Henry sent his mother some money, enclosed in a short letter. Willie Mae wrote back, thanking him for the money and for telling his overseas address. She added that she would like to hear from him more often.

One afternoon, Bro was having stomach cramps and left work early. Meanwhile at Bro's home, Thomas was spending time with Christine and his granddaughter. Bro's truck broke down less than a mile from his house. Bro left his truck and walked home. Feeling awful, and also angry because his truck had failed him, he didn't notice his father's car in the yard.

Bro walked in and found his wife and his father in an embrace. Bro grabbed his dad and hit him so hard he fell to the floor.

"Damn, daddy, do you hate me that much?"

Christine grabbed Bro, saying, "It's not your father's fault."

"What do you mean it's not his fault!?" Bro screamed, pushing Christine to the floor while holding his father around the neck. Christine reached up and grabbed a pillow from the couch, hitting Bro across his back. Bro released his father and grabbed the pillow from Christine. Fearing for Thomas' life, she begged him to leave.

Thomas, barely able to stand, was bleeding from his mouth. "No, I'm not going to leave you here with him like this."

"Please go, I can handle it," she cried as she tried pushing her father- in-law toward the door. She stood between them.

Bro thundered, "Dammit, woman! Just let me get my hands on him. I'll fix it where none of us will ever have to lay eyes on his ass again."

The baby started crying in the bedroom.

"Christine, go see after the baby," Bro shouted.

"No, Bro, I am not going to leave you and your daddy out here alone. Besides, she's okay, she's in the crib."

"Get out of my house and don't you ever step foot in here again or I'll kill you with my bare hands. Do you hear me?" Bro demanded.

"Please, Mr. Thomas, just leave us alone," cried Christine as she moved over to Bro and circled her arms around his heaving body.

"Alright. But, boy, you better not hurt this woman or I'll find you and finish what happened years ago," Thomas threatened. He stomped out and slammed the door behind him.

The baby was crying harder than ever. "Woman, get your damn hands off me." Christine backed away, out of his reach.

"Bitch! That was my father. How could you do this to me? The hell with you! Get your shit and get the fuck out!"

"Bro, I know you're hurting, but nothing happened between your daddy and me. Your dad loves you. While you were out working, building homes, your daddy would come by here every day, and help me around the house, seeing after his grandchild and me. It was me who wanted him."

"Yeah? Just you get your things and get out right now," Bro said again.

Christine and Bro split up and he immediately filed for divorce. Mrs. Willie Mae, hurt by the news, tried to speak with Bro about what happened. But Bro never told her about his father's backstabbing ways.

Henry returned from the army with some bad news. He had received a dishonorable discharge. This broke Willie Mae's heart. She asked him what happened, but he didn't want to talk about it. He said he just wanted to go back to his motel room.

Willie Mae reminded her youngest son on his daily afternoon visits that she was there for him should he want to talk about what happened. Henry refused to tell anyone, not even his brothers, why the army gave him the boot. But on the third day of his return, Henry found himself alone in the living room with his mother. In a rush of boldness, he disclosed what he called good news of his marriage to Virginia Gilmore, whom he had secretly married four months before the abrupt end of his army career. He explained to his mother that he was seeing Virginia on and off before he went into the army and that, while he was in Germany, he arranged for Virginia to fly to Germany so they could get married. He told his mother that he had saved enough money to start a married life and was not deterred from that decision even when Virginia told him she was pregnant by his former classmate, Steve Williams.

"Mom, Virginia and I are very much in love. I know you have questions about my life, the decisions that I've made, but we love one another. Isn't that what counts? Besides, no one will ever know that this child isn't my child. It's a girl and her name is Melissa Turner."

Willie Mae breathed a long sigh, releasing the tension of the unknown. She followed it with a warm smile. "Son, one day you are going to have to disclose the truth to your daughter, Melissa, but until you are ready, we'll keep silent. When can I meet them?"

Henry's face brightened up. "They are waiting outside in the car," he said. He jumped up and headed for the front door.

"Well, boy, go and bring them inside so I can see my granddaughter and catch you up with what's been going on around here."

Henry of course wasn't surprised to hear about Christine and Bro's split. The Turner house became home to Henry, Virginia, and Melissa. Rather than go out and find a job as his wife had done, he was always drinking and hanging out in the clubs playing pool. Willie Mae couldn't understand her Henry's behavior, so she continued to question him. One day, Henry stumbled into the house drunk. Willie Mae helped him to the bedroom. Henry mumbled something about seeing his dad with another woman. Willie Mae quizzed her son relentlessly until finally succeeding in getting him to tell what he saw.

The next day, Willie Mae went to her mother and told her. Frannie Mae had her daughter sit next to her on the worn, blue-velvet sofa and took hold of her hands. "Willie, I don't want to tell you what to do, but you've known for years that Thomas slept around. Though you wouldn't admit it. Now, you know that your child knows. I will never tell you what to do, but, honey, I will say this: you haven't ever had a husband, and he has never been a father. All he's been is a man laying up with my daughter, making her life and the children's life a living hell."

Willie Mae admitted. "Yes, I looked the other way for much too long." She took a long, deep breath and added, "I am going to take the kids and leave. I can't live like this anymore."

"Y'all more than welcome to come live here."

That same day, Willie Mae confronted Thomas, packed her and the children's things, and they all left to go live with her mother.

A couple of months later, Thomas moved out of their house and went to live with his girlfriend. Willie Mae and her family moved back home.

FINAL BLOW

The atmosphere at the Turner home was pleasant now that Thomas had moved out permanently. Frannie Mae spent most evenings at her daughter's house.

One evening, Thomas dropped by to see for himself about the rumor that his family had returned to the house. Upon entering the kitchen, he saw a very happy gathering with Willie Mae, Irene, Frannie, and Susan. Their expressions soon turned serious.

Irene and Susan had been coached ahead of time to be at least civil to their father when they'd see him. They said together, "Hi, Dad."

In a soft voice, Willie Mae instructed them, "Girls, go to your room." They slipped away.

Thomas gave a big grin. "What do we have here? It didn't work out living at your mama's?"

Frannie Mae jumped in and answered for her daughter. "What brings you back? Your girlfriend don' threw you out already? No, that too easy, less you come to try and pick up your things."

Thomas slapped his hands on the kitchen table as he said, "No, I came to throw you out! I never liked you anyway. You can't keep no man and neither can your daughter."

Frannie Mae pushed her chair back and stood up to face him. "I ain't going nowhere. This is as much my daughter's house as it's yours. Man like you don't know what it's like to have a real home. Your home is wherever your second head leads you."

Willie Mae yelled, "That's right, you no-good fuckin' bastard. You think you the shit, anyway."

"You just can shut your mouth!" Thomas shouted at Frannie Mae. "Willie Mae, you better tell your mama to shut up before I... I— "

"I can read your feeble mind. Before you hit me? Like you hit and beat my daughter and grandchildren? Willie Mae, you just stay right where you are. 'cause you and those chilluns ain't goin' no place."

"Woman, you better get out of my way!"

Ready with her ammunition, Frannie Mae said, "I have been wanting to tell you this for a long time. You have never been any good to yourself and nobody else. You think you a sharp, clean man who can get any woman you please. Treat 'em any old way. Well, I'm here to tell you that those days are over. Times have changed and you damn sure is not gonna be a part of those changes. I never could see what my daughter saw in you, but I'm glad to say that she damn don't see nothing now."

Thomas lurched forward a step, grabbed Mrs. Frannie Mae's left arm and slapped her with one blow, which forced her body to lean against the chair and fall over it. Landing on the floor on her back, her right leg twisted at an odd angle. Henry had entered the house just as his dad was striking his grandmother. He and Willie Mae rushed to her rescue.

Henry grabbed his father and was about to hit him, when his grandmother screamed, "Don't you dare strike your daddy! Do you hear me? Don't you dare! Leave him be! Listen, you don't want that on your conscience. You don't want to suffer in death or repent for his sins. God will take care of Thomas. I may not live to see that day, but God will take care of him. Now, Henry, turn him loose and come help your mama."

Henry let his dad go, warning him, "I won't hit you this time, only because I love my mama and grandma. You better get out of here and never come back, 'cause I can't promise you that I won't hurt you the next time. You ain't never been my daddy and never will be."

Without a word, Thomas picked his pipe up off the floor and left. Willie Mae called to Irene and Susan to come from the bedroom to help their grandma. They took Frannie Mae to the hospital emergency room. She suffered a serious back injury. The doctors said that she would always need a cane to aid her in walking. Henry never had anything to do with his father again. When Willie Mae's neighbors moved, they rented their house to the Turners to make caring for Frannie Mae easier. A month after the one-way fight,

Willie Mae filed for divorce. Thomas was not happy at all about this. He was determined to make life a living hell for Willie Mae. He blamed her mother for the downfall of their marriage and swore that he would gain ownership of their home. A trial was held and the court ruled in favor of Willie Mae keeping the house and Thomas paying child support for Irene and Susan.

Bro was determined not to be like his father and decided to give his marriage to Christine a second chance. Within a few weeks of rebuilding their relationship, they found themselves making exotic love. Once again, Bro and Christine found the true love and respect they had once shared. After the trial, Bro announced to the family that he and Christine had reconciled. Two months later, Christine and Bro remarried. Martha and Fred, on the other hand, were having marital problems. Martha continued to flirt, party, and socialize as she always had among her friends. Fred accused her of neglecting their sons. He was afraid to guess what else might be happening during her nights out.

Bertha and Will continued to have a happy family life with their four kids.

Dot, from her perspective as college student and eldest daughter, could never approve of her sister having four children, nor could she approve of her brother Henry's marriage to a woman who was six months' pregnant. Dot graduated from college, married her college classmate Charles Anderson, had a child, and became an elementary school teacher. Irene graduated from high school in 1960. Her goals were to attend college and pursue a degree in education. Susan, twelve years old and the youngest of the children, spent lots of time with her friends, enjoying after-school activities.

VIOLENCE

Louise Battle decided it was time to visit her biological father. She and her husband had raised four children. Her mother had divulged her father's name—Thomas Turner—to her years before. But Louise figured she didn't need him in her life and, in fact, got along quite well without his help. But at this stage of life, she was curious about her roots. Her children might benefit from knowing another grandfather, too.

Willie Mae answered the knock on the door and invited the young lady into her home. Louise introduced herself, explaining that her mother had told her that Thomas was indeed her father. Louise put her birth certificate into Willie Mae's hands for her to see. Willie Mae answered that they were divorced, and she didn't have any idea how she could contact him. After getting acquainted for a few minutes, Willie Mae escorted Louise to the door, stating that if she heard from Thomas, she would indeed inform him of Louise's visit. After she closed the door, feelings of anger and joy swept over Willie Mae. Her nightmare years of being married to a bastard were finally over. She wished that Thomas would burn in hell for the torment he caused her and his bastard child.

That afternoon, Willie Mae gathered her children at her home and informed them about Thomas's daughter's visit. Louise had been fathered a year after their own oldest child, Dot. The news of this out-of-wedlock daughter didn't surprise anyone. They were well aware of Thomas's infidelities. They agreed among themselves it was just a matter of time before such a person from Thomas's "other life" materialized into theirs.

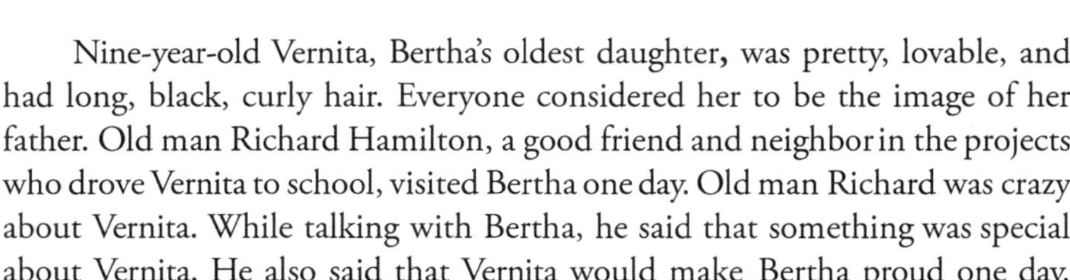

Nine-year-old Vernita, Bertha's oldest daughter, was pretty, lovable, and had long, black, curly hair. Everyone considered her to be the image of her father. Old man Richard Hamilton, a good friend and neighbor in the projects who drove Vernita to school, visited Bertha one day. Old man Richard was crazy about Vernita. While talking with Bertha, he said that something was special about Vernita. He also said that Vernita would make Bertha proud one day. Vernita had told him how she loved going to school. Bertha and Mr. Hamilton reminisced about their own years in school.

From the kitchen, Bertha poured two glasses of sweet iced tea. She raised her voice so it would carry to the living room. "Mr. Hamilton, during my era, there were no restrictions on discipline in the schools. Teachers could use a hand paddle or rubber strap. And the students recited the Pledge of Allegiance and the Lord's Prayer before class began. God was not banned from school."

Mr. Hamilton settled back in the rocking chair and said, "That's so, way back when, too."

Bertha handed him a glass and sat on the sofa. She said, "The teachers selected a student to monitor the classroom. Their job was to write down the names of disruptive students. The students also had to lay their heads on their desks whenever the teacher left the room, raising them only when she returned. Any student who got written up was punished with either the hand paddle or the rubber strap. If their behavior was beyond the teacher's control, they were sent to the principal's office. The principal used the same method of disciplinary actions as well as notifying the parents. Also, the child usually got disciplined again by the parents. Was it so in your time?"

"Sure was.... Well, Bertha from what I hear from children today, things are changing a lot, and we still got a long ways to go. But I feel that children should have bus transportation if they live a long distance from school. That's why I drive childrens to school for a small fee. Hey, where is that husband of yours Will? I haven't seen him lately. Man, I never have seen a man like him. Normally, he's here cleaning, cooking, or saying he's on his way to the groceries store. Bertha, you are damn lucky to have a man like Will."

Bertha nodded in agreement.

"Well, Bertha, I guess I'll go now. I just wanted to check on you and Will and the kids. Tell that good husband and father of your childrens that I stopped by," Mr. Hamilton said as he shut the door.

One evening while playing in an empty lot down the street, WJ, their oldest son, stepped on a nail that came through his shoe. His friend rushed to get Bertha. When Bertha got to WJ, she pulled out the nail and, in a panic, sucked some blood out of the wound. A neighbor who saw this ran to get Henry, who lived behind his sister's home. Henry pulled Bertha away and placed WJ into his neighbor's arms while he attended to his sister.

Henry had never seen his sister like this before. "Bertha, what is wrong with you? Why did you suck WJ's foot?"

Bertha murmured, "I have no idea. I was scared that he would get an infection, but I don't know what came over me to do that."

They all went back home. Henry calmed her down before calling Will.

When Will arrived, he found a delirious wife and a son in pain. It was the opinion of Mrs. Gloria, a neighbor, that WJ needed to go to the hospital and have his wound treated. Will asked his brother-in-law to stay with Bertha until his return.

As soon as Will and WJ returned from the emergency room, Henry reported that Bertha hadn't responded. "I think my sister needs to see a doctor. I called mom. She's on her way over."

Will's gaze searched his wife's face. Her eyes stared blankly into space. "Bertha, look at me baby, say something! WJ is fine. The doctor says he's going to be all right. Bertha, don't do this to us. We need you."

Bertha did not respond. Willie Mae arrived with Dot. They decided that Bertha probably had a nervous breakdown. They questioned Will about Bertha's recent behavior.

"Bertha has been acting weird lately, but I thought that she was just tired."

They took Bertha to the hospital. The doctors confirmed that she had a nervous breakdown. She was transferred to the veterans' hospital. The children, of course, were well taken care of by their father during her absence.

Will had a lot to deal with. One major item, to Vernita, was that she had problems with the way her father styled her hair. So instead of hurting her father's feelings, she asked her older friend, Sandra Moreland, to fix her hair before she went to school.

Sandra obliged, but didn't understand the problem. "Vernita, why don't you just tell your father that you don't like the way he combs your hair?"

"I don't want to break my father's heart. Besides, my mother should be back soon. He doesn't have to know. I can come by your house before I leave for school. That way, he will never know."

Will visited Sandra's house to ask her parents if she could escort Vernita and her cousin Melissa (Henry and Virginia Turner's eight-year-old daughter), to school. Sandra's parents agreed that she could. Vernita and Melissa enjoyed walking to school together. It made them feel independent. Melissa, however, was very shy. Sandra was aware of this and was very protective of her. On their way to school, Sandra, Vernita, and Melissa would have to pass by the Finneys' property down the street from their school.

The Finneys were a rowdy family with thirteen children. The kids, overall, had a bad reputation in the schools and neighborhood. The family depended on welfare and their mother was a foul-mouthed alcoholic. She was very protective of her children, though, and had been known to threaten to shoot anyone who tried to harm them. Bernard Finney, one of the youngest kids, had a reputation that took him to the police department.

One day after school, Sandra had basketball practice. She asked Vernita and Melissa to see how they felt about walking home alone.

Vernita assured her, "Melissa and I will be all right."

"Are you sure y'all don't mind walking home by yourselves? I'm sure the coach wouldn't mind y'all staying here till practice is over."

"No, I rather go home." "Me too," Melissa piped in.

"Alright…. but remember, go straight home and don't talk to any strangers," Sandra lectured.

They headed home after school. The girls decided not to go through the tunnel, a student pathway built for safe crossing to avoid the heavy traffic. Several students had been raped in the tunnel. One of them was a friend of Melissa's. Melissa refused to walk through the tunnel, even knowing that the school had assigned a crossing patrol since the incidents. The girls took their chances and carefully crossed the highway. Several students who had used the tunnel walked along with them. After five minutes, Melissa noticed that the Bible was missing from her book bag. She yelled for Vernita to wait until she went back and found her book. Bernard Finney had tagged along behind Melissa. When he saw Melissa pick up a Bible and not a textbook, he started teasing her.

Vernita rushed to Melissa's side and told her to ignore him. "Just kept walking, do you hear me? We are almost home."

"I'm scared."

Bernard taunted, "Hey, holy roller sanctified, that Bible ain't gonna help you none."

"I'm getting tired of your mouth, Bernard. Why don't you just go home and leave us alone."

"You think you're bad, huh!" He pushed Vernita. "Melissa, pick up your book bag and go home."

Melissa ran home to get her mother. Meanwhile, Bernard continued to pick a fight with Vernita.

Vernita stood her ground. She warned Bernard, "I don't want to fight with you. But I ain't gonna let you pick on me. You like picking on people. I may not beat your butt, but I ain't afraid either. I don't mind you picking on me, but I just hate it when you pick on my cousin."

Melissa's mother arrived in time to prevent them from fighting. "Vernita, get your things, and you, son, go on about your business and leave this girl alone."

Melissa's mother informed Will about the incident. Will and Virginia worked out an arrangement for transportation for the girls when Sandra would have basketball practice in the future.

Bernard confronted Vernita at school the next day. Vernita ignored him and, eventually, he left her alone. Bernard looked around for other prey. He started harassing Mrs. Quanita Lawson's son, Chuck. Almost daily, he would corner him in the hallway and take his money, threatening to beat him if he didn't hand it over. Mrs. Lawson was a religious lady. Her husband pastored the Holiness Church, and violence was against their religion. Fearing that Bernard would follow through with his threats, Chuck continued to hand over the money.

One day at school, Chuck was finally pushed once too many and fought back. Bernard and Chuck were both escorted to the principal's office. Their parents were phoned. Quanita Lawson immediately drove to the school to discuss her son's involvement in the fight. The principal related to her what happened. He also told her that Bernard was a problem child, always getting into trouble. He assured her that Chuck was just defending himself.

Mrs. Lawson was shocked to hear this. She told the principal, "No matter what happened here today, my son knows that violence is not the way to solve things."

Quanita escorted Chuck to their car. She then drove to the Finney's home, and insisted that Chuck stay in the car while she talked to Mrs. Finney. Quanita's intention was to have a friendly conversation with the boy's parents, hoping to resolve the matter. Meanwhile, Mrs. Finney was watching from her window as Quanita walked toward the house. Bernard saw her too, and told his mother who Mrs. Lawson was, and his quick version of the reason for her visit.

"Bernard, get me my gun!"

Bernard scurried to grab the handgun from the kitchen drawer near the stove and gave it to his mother. Mrs. Lawson approached the house and knocked on the door of Mrs. Finney's front porch.

Mrs. Finney couldn't believe that Mrs. Lawson would dare confront her about something one of her kids had done. In her usual way, she yelled through the door, "I don't have a damn thing to say to you, bitch!"

"Mrs. Finney, I'm Chuck's mother, Quanita. I just want to discuss our sons' fighting one another at school. Would you o—"

Before Quanita could finish, Mrs. Finney, in a frenzy of drunken rage, opened the door, waving her arms in the air. "Bitch, I told you that I didn't have anything to say!" She then lowered her arms, pointed the gun at Quanita, and fired. Quanita fell down dead on the porch.

Chuck screamed from the car as several more shots rang out. "No! Mom! Please stop shooting! Please, somebody help us… please!"

The neighbors called the police. Mrs. Finney and her son were taken to the police station. Quanita was pronounced dead upon arrival at the hospital. The community was in an uproar over this tragedy.

Quanita Lawson's murder changed the lives of her family and friends. But not Mrs. Finney's, she didn't even go to prison. She had accused Mrs. Lawson of causing a disturbance on her property. Even though no additional weapon was found near Mrs. Lawson, Mrs. Finney insisted that she was just defending herself. The jury found her not guilty. Yet everyone knew that Quanita Lawson was a religious lady who didn't believe in violence.

Quanita's death was not soon forgotten in the neighborhood. People shied away from any type of confrontation with their neighbors. They found

Mrs. Finney murdered a month later. Her body was found in a neighboring alley, stabbed to death. The police report stated that the body was dumped there after she had been killed. The killer was never found. Bertha returned home from the hospital, feeling rested. Family members finally told her of Quanita's fatal tragedy. Church services were never the same. Quanita's original songs were sung every week and brought about a deeper spiritual movement among the congregation. Six months later, Reverend Lawson and his family moved away.

POISONED MIND

Will and Henry researched ways to make extra income and decided to make home brew and sell it. They liked malt liquor best. They planned on hosting home parties every weekend and selling dinners at these parties from the club they had joined. But Will's always being in the public eye caused problems in his marriage. He started clubbing on a regular basis. He asked Bertha to join him, but she always declined. She didn't want to leave their children alone at home. The children were, the least, of Will's concerns. Will had begun to drink heavily and stayed out all night. Peer pressure was getting the best of him. Bertha and Will argued and fought continuously. Until one day, Bertha decided to leave. She and the children moved in with her mother, who had remarried.

Their grandmother, Frannie Mae, had taken ill and couldn't handle living alone in the rented house. She had moved in with Willie Mae and her new husband, Mr. Vinson, at his house. Mr. Vinson was a weird old man. The children couldn't agree what was worse: He wouldn't allow any lights on after seven PM except the kitchen light. The children had to do their homework in the hallway by the reflection of that one light. Also, he'd cook hot, spicy food and force everyone to eat it or go without any food. Willie Mae went along with his rules to keep the peace. Bertha didn't like the man, but respected him for the sake of her mother.

Martha and Fred's marriage fell apart. Fred got fed up with his wife's attention to her male friends and the neglect of their sons. Hanging out with her friends was all that was on her mind. Fred left without warning and moved to Florida. Within nine months, Martha got an uncontested divorce and married again, to Ned Poole, a long-time friend. She left the boys with her mother until she and Ned got settled in New Jersey where Ned lived.

The Vinson household grew larger. Bro had started drinking heavily and hanging out with his colleagues. Christine discovered that Bro had a one-night affair and kicked him out of the house, throwing his clothes out the window behind him.

Mr. Vinson was furious with the increasing number of people in the house but didn't let his wife know. Instead, in his quiet way, he insisted on doing all the cooking and cleaning. His wife's home care of her ill mother occupied most of her time. Although it made no difference, Willie Mae's children and grandchildren complained to her about Mr. Vinson's food, which was always very hot, spicy, and greasy.

Frannie Mae's illness got worse. She worried what would happen to her grandchildren if she died. Lying in her bed, she had many quiet conversations with her daughter. "Willie Mae, your baby is going to bring you a lot of pain. Out of all your children, Susan will burden you the most. I may not be here to see it, but I feel that she's the worst. But Bertha… God bless her… will always be at your side."

Frannie Mae became weaker. Fred Junior sat faithfully at his grandmother's bedside and was there when she gradually became speechless and fainted. They rushed her to the hospital. The initial news of her condition lifted their spirits. Everyone prayed she would recover.

The situation caused Bertha to become so irate that she openly blamed her stepfather's spicy food for her grandmother's illness. Her grandma started to recover on the fifth day in the hospital. She could sit up and talk. Then, suddenly, she suffered another setback, and slipped into a coma.

Bertha again accused her stepfather, this time to his face. "If she don't make it, it's cause of you!"

Mr. Vinson's temper finally erupted. He yelled, "What the hell do you mean it's because of me? I haven't done nothing but tried to keep a roof over you all heads. Hell, and I'm damn tired of this shit!"

When Willie Mae and Dot returned from the hospital, Susan was washing dishes. In the living room, Willie Mae told everyone that there wasn't any change in grandma's condition. She was still in a coma. Suddenly, Susan screamed from the kitchen. Mr. Vinson and Willie Mae ran in to see what was wrong.

"I just saw grandma. She was standing outside, looking at me through the window."

Willie Mae put her arms around her daughter. "Sit down, Susan. You been standing on your feet too long."

"But, Mom, I swear I saw grandma. She was looking at me through the kitchen window."

The phone rang and Bertha hurried to answer it. It was the hospital, calling to notify the family that grandma had passed away.

Bertha screamed, "Lord, no…. Mama! Grandma is dead… she's gone!"

Everyone cried and embraced one another for comfort. Mr. Vinson attended to his wife, who pined over the loss of her beloved mother.

Mr. Vinson concerned himself with the preparation of meals for his wife and family and friends who came to show their respect. When she was out shopping for a dress for her grandma's funeral, Bertha happened to see Mr. Vinson. Hiding among the crowd, she watched Mr. Vinson talking to an attractive elderly lady. The lady had a quick look around then placed what looked like a bottle of food seasoning in his hands. He dropped it in his pocket.

Later, Bertha questioned Mr. Vinson on his whereabouts that day. He claimed to have gone shopping for their mother. Bertha knew that was a lie. They had already been shopping.

Mr. Vinson prepared breakfast the day of the funeral. Again, the family complained that the food was too spicy. Later on, they complained about having nervous stomachs, but believed it was because of their emotions. Vernita got ill in the car on the way to the church and vomited all over herself. When they got to the church, a neighbor took Vernita to her house to clean her up.

Everyone was gathered at the church for the funeral. The ceremonies began but came to a halt when Bertha walked up to the casket and tried to pick up her grandmother's body. As soon as they saw that, her brothers rushed up the aisle to calm her down and escort her to her seat.

"Grandma is resting now, Bertha. She's tired. Let her sleep."

Everyone returned to the Vinson home after the funeral. Bertha lied across her deceased grandmother's bed. Willie Mae was afraid she was having a nervous breakdown.

Two weeks later, Mr. Vinson was still cooking his spicy food and forcing it upon the family. By his rules, it was still lights out at seven and the television was only allowed on for a few hours each day.

Bertha exploded when she saw her daughter doing homework in the bathroom. It was the only room allowed a light on. She ran to the kitchen and grabbed Mr. Vinson by the shirt. "You ain't no damn good! Mama, he's trying to kill us! Don't you think it's funny that he's always doing the cooking? His food is too spicy, making us eat all of it, not leaving a crumb on our plates. Why don't you tell mama about the food seasoning your girlfriend gave you? You don't keep it in the cupboard. Cause I checked…. Mama, I'm tired of him cooking his poisoning food!"

"Bertha, turn him loose!"

"No, I want… I want to kill him."

Willie Mae yelled at Bro to help her with Bertha. "Bro, come talk to your sister."

Bro hovered near Bertha. "Mom, Bertha is right. The food *is* too hot and spicy. My stomach haven't been right since I moved in here."

Bertha let Mr. Vinson go. He stepped back and smoothed out his clothes. In a calm voice, he said, "Willie Mae, you and your children have until noon tomorrow to get out of my house. Now, if you and Susan want to stay, y'all can, but I ain't going to put up with this anymore."

Mr. Vinson left for the remainder of the day. Willie Mae called Dot and informed her of what had happened. Dot's girlfriend, Charlotte, a realtor, told her of an apartment immediately available. Dot arranged for the family to move there. All the family moved out of Mr. Vinson's, never to return.

A NEW LOVE

A month later, Mr. Vinson's first wife's sister visited Willie Mae. She had seen the obituary in the newspaper. She revealed the long-suffering death of her sister, whose death was similar to that of Willie Mae's mother.

The lady mentioned an insurance policy that Mr. Vinson received the benefit from when his wife died. Willie Mae realized from the woman's story that the man who claimed to love her was psychotic and that she would be his next victim.

But Willie Mae later figured that he had needed to change his plans once her mother moved in with them. Willie Mae was very dependent on him to help with her mother. This delayed his plans. Then as the family grew, instead of killing one, he had to come up with a plan to wipe out everyone living in his home. The food he had cooked contained an herbal root poison—the same kind that killed her mother and would have killed her children. But, thanks to Bertha, it never happened.

This was the era of civil rights leader Martin Luther King Jr., a Baptist minister who spoke out against the violence and segregation that permeated American society. African-Americans were called Coloreds and Negroes. Their employment and educational opportunities were limited. Separate was not equal. The mission of Martin Luther King Jr. and other civil rights leaders was to make White America see that under the constitution, Negroes were entitled to equal opportunities in employment and education. James Brown, the popular soul singer, recorded a song entitled "Say

It Loud, I'm black and I'm Proud" that inspired black Americans to take pride in themselves. Vernita and her sister and brothers would dance for hours in the living room to the song.

Bertha, hearing James Brown's song, "I Feel Good," stopped by the room and said, "Y'all are playing my song."

"Mom, you heard James Brown's record?" "Sure, I listen to it all the time."

"It's bad. Mom, you look pretty," Vernita observed.

Susan added, "Yuh, Bertha, you have lost a lot of weight since you and Will separated."

"Well, guess what. I've gotten me a new boyfriend. His name is Daryl Stevenson. He's something else! You talkin' 'bout fine? He's fine, honey! He's on his way over. Now, I want y'all to treat him nice. Vernita, I want you to make sure your sister and brothers have on some clean clothes. And straighten up this house."

Daryl arrived and Bertha introduced him to the family. After he had mingled with everybody, they left on their date. They went to the club and had a great time dancing the night away.

Will was well aware of Bertha's new social life. And he was jealous of this Daryl, who he called scum. Will decided he wanted Bertha back. After all, he figured, they were only separated, not divorced. Seeing her reminded Will of when they first met, how beautiful she was.

Though Daryl used and dealt in drugs, he managed to keep this secret from Bertha. Until one night, Daryl invited Bertha to his place. Arriving there, they found the place overrun with Daryl's friends. They were playing a poker and appeared very comfortable in Daryl's apartment. Bertha could smell a strong, strange scent. She thought the men must be smoking some funny-smelling foreign cigarettes. She also saw the men drinking whisky straight from bottles sitting on the table.

While the men continued playing cards, Rodney asked them if they wanted to play, which made Daryl furious.

"Hey, man, if we wanted to play, don't you think we would ask?" shouted Daryl. Rodney didn't catch on. He was feeling drunk and friendly. "Hey man, what's up?

Y'all back already? Excuse me, please!" Rodney said to Bertha. He passed an appreciative gaze at her body. "Would you like for me to get you something to drink or smoke?"

"I'm sorry, I don't smoke."

"Hey, mama, that's cool with me."

Daryl cut in, "Hey, man, I don't need you offering my lady anything to drink. I can do that myself. What up with this? I thought y'all was going to a party."

"We did go, but the lady was in a bitchy mood, so we left." Daryl went to the kitchen to see who was there.

Bertha asked, "So what are y'all playing?"

"Do you know how to play spades or blackjack?" "I know a little."

"Then why don't you pull up a chair."

"No, baby, we're not going to stay," Daryl answered for her. "It's late and I'm gonna take you home. They'll be here all night. Besides, baby, you got to go to work in the morning."

"You're right. I'm sorry, I'll catch y'all another time."

"Wait here, baby. I'll get your coat" Daryl said.

The doorbell rang. To Bertha's surprise, it was someone she knew—Josephine, an old girlfriend of hers. She looked bad. Her clothes hung off her shoulders, and something obviously had her high. She was with one of Daryl's buddies.

"Bertha Turner! Is that you? Girl, I haven't seen you in a long time." "Well, I haven't seen you in some time either."

Josephine asked, "So, what brings you to these parts?"

"Oh, I'm here with Daryl."

Josephine raised an eyebrow. "Daryl… you didn't tell me you were seeing Bertha. Now, you better treat this girl right. Last I heard, her daddy was a cop."

Daryl wrapped his arms around Bertha.

Bertha said, "Well, daddy and mama divorced."

As Rodney and his gang were leaving, he called out, "Hey, Daryl, man, we are going to split, since y'all can't decide on what y'all going to do." The door slammed behind them.

Daryl released her and offered her a kitchen chair. "You didn't tell me your daddy was a cop," a surprised Daryl said. "cause my daddy ain't no cop no more. He got fired. Besides, my daddy remarried and left town. I haven't seen Josephine in years. She ran away from home, the last I heard. She looks bad. So what's up with my daddy being a cop?"

"Oh, nothing. Let me help you with your coat," he said, then rushed to the kitchen table and grabbed his keys. Walking back toward Bertha, Daryl stared intently at her. She recognized and welcomed the lust in his eyes. Daryl hugged her tight and kissed her lips, nose, cheeks, neck, and right ear as he escorted her from the apartment into his car.

Before starting the engine, he pulled her close, kissing her softly, deeply, and whispered, "I love you, Bertha." They finally broke from the passionate embrace, and he drove her home.

Two weeks later, the police department found Josephine dead. Someone had shot her up with an overdose of heroin and shoved a soda bottle up in her vagina. Whoever did this to her was a sick, vicious person. Though Josephine had run away from home years before, many of her friendsand family members went to the funeral to pay their respects.

Soon after, Will met Bertha at work and asked her about Josephine's death. They shared their feelings about Josephine's tragedy. Will told Bertha about Daryl's drug connections. But Bertha didn't believe him.

"Will, you're just jealous. I've never seen him with drugs."

"That's because he knows you don't get off. Mark my word, he's not right for you. You better be careful."

One evening, after Daryl and Bertha had sex, she examined his body while he slept. She found many needle marks on his body. When he woke up, Bertha questioned him about the marks. He told her he was a diabetic, which Bertha didn't believe. She questioned him further, asking him how much insulin he took. And again Daryl lied. Knowing that Daryl was deceiving her, she dressed and asked him to take her home. Once they got to Bertha's house, Daryl kissed her passionately, and Bertha responded, not letting Daryl know that it was over between them.

She avoided his phone calls and lunch invitations. Eventually, he got the message and stopped pursing her. A couple of months later, friends found Daryl dead in his apartment. He had overdosed from cocaine.

REUNITED TRAGEDY

Daryl's death upset Bertha. Even though their relationship had ended months before, Bertha still had deep feelings for him. She discussed Daryl's death with the family and told them that Daryl's drug use was the reason their relationship had ended. Daryl's death also saddened Vernita, but at the same time, she was glad that his relationship with her mother was over.

Hoping for a reconciliation between Will and Bertha, Martha wrote a letter to her mother, inquiring about Bertha. She also told her about her marital problems with Ned and that their financial problems were so overwhelming she had no choice but to move the family back home.

Bertha and Will became close friends again. He began spending more time with his family. He asked Bertha to consider reuniting with him in marriage. Bertha revealed to Will her feelings about Daryl, and requested time to think about Will's offer. Months later, Bertha and Will remarried. They purchased a home. This symbolized a new beginning for them. Will got a part-time job at night and insisted that Bertha quit her job.

Fred Cleveland returned from Florida. Martha returned home and rekindled her relationship with Fred. They had never divorced, and within months, they reunited their family. Fred knew that Martha was still very close to her twin sister. As a surprise, he contacted a realtor who would tip him off first about any house that would come up for sale in Bertha and Will's neighborhood, so the twins could live near one another.

Some people in Will and Bertha's neighborhood had spotted a naked white man roaming around their streets. One night, a neighbor claiming to have seen this man visited Bertha. Minutes after he arrived, they all heard somebody scream, "Wow! It's the butt-naked man!"

Everyone opened their doors or peeked out their windows to see a naked man running down the street.

Later that night, Bertha told Will about the stranger. Her husband's reaction puzzled Bertha. She thought Will would express some concern for her safety, but his only response was silence. The next day, Bertha called Martha and recounted the incident about the neighborhood madman and Will's laid back attitude. When Martha shared this news with Fred, he contacted his realtor and cancelled the plans to relocate his family in Bertha's neighborhood.

Will stayed out later and later, not coming home after work, and only spending time with his family on Sundays. Bertha didn't know that Will had met a nice-looking lady—one he had grown fond of. Spending time at home no longer was a priority for him. He found the nightlife too exciting. His girlfriend loved to party.

He sometimes asked Bertha to go out with him. "Bertha, Vernita is old enough to babysit the kids. We're only going out for a couple of hours."

"You can go. I wouldn't enjoy myself knowing they're here by themselves."

"Well, you can sit here and worry about these kids by yourself. I'll be damned if I'm going to sit here with you and not have fun just cause I'm married. Hell! You went out when you lived with your mama."

"I should have known, you haven't change a bit. You ain't told me nothin' but lies. You promised me that it would be different. But you love the streets. Who in the hell is she?"

"Woman, you're crazy. There you go accusing me of having another woman again. Your mama's been acting strange lately. Does she know who she is?"

"Damn it, answer me!" Bertha insisted.

"Bertha, damn it! Now, you're taking this a little too far. What the hell is wrong with you? You're having a nervous breakdown, that's it."

"The hell I'm having a nervous breakdown. You want me to have one so you can move your bitch in here. I'm sorry to have to disappoint you, 'cause it ain't gonna happen. I know what I'm talking about."

Tired of arguing, Will finished dressing and left. The phone rang. Vernita had watched her parents from the hallway.

"It's Will's mother," Vernita said.

"Will just left," Bertha told Vernita. Before she could relay this message, Bertha took the phone.

"Oh, then he must be on his way over," his mother said.

"No, I don't think so. He's on his way to the club."

"Bertha, you sound angry. Have you and Will been arguing?"

"Has he been telling you we've been arguing?" Bertha accused.

"No, he hasn't. Well, tell him I called."

"OK."

In tears, Bertha slammed the phone down. Vernita came into the room. "Mom, are you are all right?"

"What are you doing up, Vernita?"

"I heard you and dad fighting."

"Now, don't you go worrying about me and your daddy arguing. We just had a little misunderstanding. Go and get back in bed."

"Mom, can I sleep in your bed till daddy comes home?"

Bertha hugged her and said, "Sure, baby, you just climb into my bed. Mama needs some company."

Shortly afterward, Bertha heard voices in the front yard. Bertha saw all three of the occupants in the car from her living room window. Will was drunk. His girlfriend's father had driven him home, and the girlfriend was along for the ride. When Will finally came into the house, Bertha pretended to be asleep. Seeing his daughter in his bed, Will slept on the couch.

It was Father's Day. Bertha and the children served Will his breakfast in bed. Henry stopped by the house that morning to show off his Father's Day gift. Will, in turn, showed him the pocketknife WJ had given him.

Will asked, "Man, you wanna exchange knives?"

"What you talking about? How are you gonna explain this to your son when he asks you what you did with his knife?"

"Let me worry about that. Are you gonna give me the knife or what?"

"Will, what have you gone and got yourself into this time?"

"Nothing, man I've just been working too hard."

"Yeah, I heard. You need to spend time with your family. You know, that's my sister you're married to."

"Hey, man, you ain't fixin' to butt in my business."

"No, I just care about both of you, that's all. Here, you can have my knife and keep your son's, too."

"Hey, thanks."

Weeks later while doing laundry, Bertha found the knife in the pocket of a pair of his pants. *What is he doing with this?* Bertha wondered. She hid the knife in her hatbox.

That night, Will came home very late. Bertha woke up when she heard car brakes squeaking to a stop. She got out of bed and peeked out the window. She saw a woman and a man in the front seat of the car. Could it be her husband necking with his girlfriend? Staring out the window, she could also see a man sitting in the back seat. Bertha woke Vernita to confirm what she saw. And what she saw shocked her daughter.

"Mama! Who's that woman dad is kissing?"

Bertha pulled Vernita from the window to take another look. "Oh, baby, don't worry. That's probably a close friend of your father. You can go and get back into bed." She kissed Vernita on the forehead and escorted her back to her room.

Vernita, concerned about her mother, didn't go back to sleep. Instead, she intended to stand at the bedroom door and listen to their conversation.

Will finally got out of the car. Moore Lawson, Will's girlfriend's father, got out of the back seat and sat in the driver's seat. As Will ambled to the door, Bertha opened it for him.

Bertha didn't care if she woke the neighbors. She shouted, "Will, don't you dare bring your ass into my house!"

Mr. Lawson didn't drive off; he and his daughter remained in the car, with the windows down. Will continued walking up the steps. "What the hell you talking about? Woman, this is my house," Will said as he pushed his way past her into the house.

They carried on, swearing at each other for at least five minutes. Vernita heard it all while watching the alarm clock minutes change. Wanting to put an end to it, she came out of her bedroom. Will saw her and demanded that she go back to her room.

Vernita confronted him. "No, I'm not going back to bed. Not with you and mama arguing like this."

"Don't you love us anymore?" Bertha asked.

Vernita stood in between them. Will shouted for Vernita to go to her room. By then, Bertha had slipped away and grabbed the knife from its hiding place. She returned and stood behind her daughter. Barely passing the knife under Vernita's arms that were raised trying to push her father away, Bertha managed to stab Will in the stomach. Will reached for Bertha, pushing his daughter aside. Bertha ran out of the house through the back door, still clutching the knife.

WJ awoke with a start at the noise and rushed to the kitchen. "Are you all right?" he asked Vernita.

"Yeah, mom and dad are fighting again."

Out the back door, they could see Will chasing after Bertha. Moments later, Will came in, panting and holding his stomach.

Moore Lawson came in the front door and found his way to the lights in the kitchen. "Man, what's going on in here? We could hear y'all arguing from way out in the car."

Will was slumped in a kitchen chair. He muttered, "Bertha and I got into it." Moore said, "Look, you're bleeding!"

"What?"

"In the stomach."

"Man, shit, I been stabbed!" "Daddy, you're bleeding," WJ cried.

"WJ, you and your sister go to y'all bedrooms."

They didn't budge. Moore sat down at the table. "Will, you need to go to the hospital."

"No, I need to get my hands on that woman of mine."

Moore moved the chair closer to Will, pointing to his gut. "Man, listen! You are bleeding."

Will explained to the children that he had to go to the hospital, and for them not to worry. He told Vernita to call his mother and ask her to look after them. Moore helped him to the car. Vernita looked out the window and saw a woman embracing Will as he got into the car.

Vernita called her Grandma Willie.

WJ was confused. "But daddy told you to call his mother."

"I don't care what he said. I'm calling my other grandma."

Willie Mae and Bro arrived within fifteen minutes. "What the hell happened here?" they asked in unison, seeing the large spots of blood on the floor.

"Grandma! Mom and dad got into a big fight. Mom stabbed daddy and ran out the back door."

"Calm down, Vernita! Bro, go and see if you can find your sister. I want you kids to pack your things. Y'all are coming with me."

Bertha entered the house.

Willie Mae rushed and grabbed her daughter, sitting her down just as she nearly collapsed. "What in the hell happened here? Where have you been?"

"Mom, I hid in the bushes out back. I stabbed Will. I don't know what came over me. I just couldn't take it no more."

"Bro is out looking for you and Henry is on his way over here. I'm taking you and the kids with me. You need to get some of your things. Never mind that, you're shaking. Tell me where your clothes are so I can pack for you. We'll come back later to get the rest," Willie Mae said.

Vernita said, "Grandma, I can pack mama's things." "All right, but let's make haste."

Bro met Henry outside. They were relieved to see their sister safe in the house. Bertha and the children packed enough for a few days and they all drove off.

THE TRIAL

Two days later, the police appeared at Willie Mae's door with a warrant for Bertha's arrest. Bertha had seen them when they drove up and willingly went with them to the police station. Willie Mae assured her daughter that they would get her out of jail. Willie Mae collected the bail money for Bertha's release. Everyone expected Will to be angry about the stabbing, but they didn't expect him to file charges against his wife. His children would be the ones to suffer.

The trial was scheduled for a month later. The court subpoenaed the children to testify. Will couldn't believe his children were going along with this. Bertha knew that putting the kids on the witness stand was the only way for her to clear herself of the charges Will had filed.

Vernita told the dreadful history of her parents' years of arguments and physical abuse. She revealed stories that neither Bertha nor Will were aware their daughter knew. She then told the story of the night of the incident.

She described to the court that she saw her father kissing and hugging another woman. She also said she had seen the stabbing. It startled Will to hear his daughter testifying against him. He then knew why his daughter telephoned Willie Mae and not his mother.

The judge found Bertha innocent of all charges.

Will confronted the children and Bertha outside the courtroom. "I know your mother and grandma put you up to this. I want you to know that I still love you."

"Daddy, what I said in the courtroom was true. I will never forgive or forget. But I will always love you, too."

WJ pulled on her arm, and said, "Come, Vernita, mama and grandma are waiting."

They were at the end of the hall. Will raised his voice for them to hear: "You and your mama have turned my kids against me."

"No, you did it all by yourself," Bertha shouted back.

Bro had built a home for his mother and Bertha and the children moved in with her. After Bertha had taken a couple more weeks off, she went back to work at the hospital.

Susan, Willie Mae's youngest child, was a junior in high school when integration was given top priority in schools across the nation. Dr. King's dream finally became reality. Harold Johnson became a focal point for Susan. Harold was tall, broad shouldered, and sported a big, beautiful Afro. This was also the era of Super Fly and cars jacked up in the rear, riding on white-rimmed tires.

Susan and Harold dated for three years. And although deeply in love, their relationship experienced many problems. Foremost was that Harold was handsome and many women pursued him. Susan constantly confronted Harold with her assumptions of his relationships with other women, which kept her upset. Susan went away to college after graduating from high school. To her surprise, her love for Harold got stronger even though they were apart. When she came home for spring break, Harold asked Susan to marry him. She accepted, married, and never returned to college.

FRIENDLY FIRE

Integration in schools, and equal opportunities in employment and housing, were finally beginning to mesh in America. The government was enforcing new laws. This change presented many challenging opportunities for minority Americans. However, integration increased violence among the races in the neighborhoods. Inner and outer city riots occurred in many cities all across the nation. Black and white gangs formed to protect each other from one another. Violence between whites and blacks caused many tragedies—injuries and death.

Many whites moved out further from the inner city rather than send their children to a predominantly black school in a mixed neighborhood. Those that could afford it sent their children to private and catholic schools.

The first couple of years were rough. But as the years passed, people began accepting the changes a little more. Yet racism still existed then, as now, in America.

The Turner grandchildren were teenagers in this new and enlightened era. Vernita attended a mixed high school and fell in love with a classmate named Floyd Davis, a black guy who was facing many family problems. Everyone gossiped about his mother being a lesbian. This bothered Floyd so much that he turned to drugs for relief. Dap was his friend and classmate who was a drug pusher and user. He exposed Floyd to the dark side of life. Dap sold marijuana, "just a herb, man…" to the users at school.

Vernita noticed a change in Floyd's behavior, though she was unaware of drugs or the effect it had on people. One day at school, during lunch, she questioned him about the letter V tattooed on his left hand. Floyd claimed that it symbolized his love for her.

"No, you had this V on your hand long before we met," she reminded him.

Floyd then told her about a previous relationship with a girl named Vanessa. He said they broke up because Vanessa's mother didn't approve of their relationship.

One evening, Floyd came home and found his mother embracing her friend Mrs. Williams on the living room sofa.

Floyd threw his keys onto the coffee table. He demanded, "What's going on here?"

The women sat up. "Excuse me, son! Where do you get off using that language?"

"Excuse me, Mom! What's going on here?"

"Nothing's going on. Mrs. Williams was just leaving."

She turned to her friend. "I apologize for my son's behavior."

Mrs. Williams smiled. "Oh, don't worry about that."

Not wanting to be in their presence any longer than he had to, Floyd scooped up his keys and ran to his bedroom, slamming the door behind him.

"So, you'll call me later?"

"Yeah, I'll do that," Mrs. Williams assured her as she left.

Floyd's mom entered his bedroom. "Now, are you going to tell me what's wrong with you?"

"Nothing's wrong with me. Why does *she* always have to be here? Why do you spend so much time with her? You and dad never do anything together anymore."

"Your daddy works most of the time. Besides, Mrs. Williams and I are just friends. I don't know what's gotten into you, boy, but you better change your ways before I change them for you."

"Yeah, right!" Floyd said as he covered his face with a pillow, signaling that the conversation was over.

Floyd, torn, hurt and confused, decided to invite his friends over while his parents were out. Nine kids showed up, high and loaded down with herb. They smoked some more before deciding to go outside where Dap pulled out a gun and showed it off.

"Where did you get that?"

"Gary, I been had this gun. I have to protect myself from my enemies. No one fucks with me and gets away with it. "Can I see it?" Gary asked.

"Yeah," Dap answered.

"This is a nice piece." Gary started playing around with the gun. Dap screamed, "Man, be careful, it's loaded!"

The warning came too late—Gary had already squeezed the trigger. The bullet ricocheted and hit Floyd who stood next to Gary. Neighbors heard the shot and called the police. Dap, Gary, and the others jumped into their cars and sped off, leaving a wounded, bleeding Floyd lying in the driveway. The police and an ambulance arrived and rushed Floyd to the hospital.

The next afternoon, Carolyn, a neighbor of Floyd's, telephoned Vernita and told her that Floyd had been shot. She offered to drive her to the hospital. When they arrived, they found Floyd's mother and his former girlfriend Vanessa sitting at his bedside. Floyd was unconscious. Vernita asked Floyd's mother about his condition.

"He was lucky. The doctor removed the bullet from his jaw. He's going to have to wear braces for a while. Here, let me get you all a chair."

"That's all right, we just stopped by for a minute. We have school tomorrow."

"I want to thank you girls for coming. I'll tell Floyd you were here."

As soon as they had walked a short distance down the hallway from Floyd's hospital room, Carolyn wrapped her arm around Vernita's and whispered to her, "Why did you leave? Floyd loves you! He's told me so."

Carolyn, I couldn't stay there with Vanessa there, too! Don't you know how I feel?"

"Sure, I know how you feel! That's why I'm telling you that you should be there, not her. They're finished, and Floyd is gonna be mad when he finds out *she* was there."

"Well, I'm not going to worry about Vanessa. I'm just glad that he's going to be okay," Vernita said as they walked to Carolyn's car.

FATAL LOVE

The police grilled Floyd about the incident. Floyd explained that it was an accident, insisting some friends of his were playing around when the gun went off, not mentioning that Dap was there when the shooting occurred. Dap called Floyd at home and threatened his life if he didn't stick to his story.

Carolyn went to see Floyd at his home. She told him that both Vernita and Vanessa were at his bedside while he was in the hospital.

This news infuriated Floyd. "That explains why Vernita didn't call me. You must think I was playing her."

"No," Carolyn assured him. "Vernita was hurt, but I told her that you were in love with her, not Vanessa."

"Thanks, Carolyn."

"What are friends for? I think that Vernita is the best thing that ever happened to you. I wish you luck." She gave him a quick, friendly hug.

Floyd stood up and walked toward the phone. "Thanks, I'm going to need it. Do you think she would speak to me if I called her?"

"Hey, you won't know till you try."

As soon as Carolyn left his house, Floyd called Vernita, telling her what happened to him, explaining that he didn't know Vanessa would be at his bedside. He repeatedly told her that he loved only her.

Vernita could not hold back her feelings. She blurted out, "How can you be in love with me when you continue to be involved with Vanessa? I wonder, do you even know the meaning of love? I have tried to understand your relationship with her, but it's very hard for me to get past my jealousy if she's always there for you. Love is based on trust, and I don't know if we have that—

or if we ever did! I got a lot of thinking to do right now about how I feel, and whether or not I want to continue this relationship."

As she requested, he agreed to give her a week without any phone calls.

Floyd's parents bought him a new car. On day seven, Floyd called Vernita and asked her out. When she saw the new car, she whistled. "Hey, I dig this car!"

"You do?" he said, following behind her, with his hands in his pockets.

"Yeah! It's bad. Your parents are letting you drive their new car?"

"Well, not exactly."

Vernita's gaze whipped from the car to Floyd. "What do you mean? Don't tell me they don't know you have their car."

"No, it's mine."

"It's yours? Gee, that's even better!"

Vernita awarded Floyd with an unexpected hug and a kiss to express her congratulations. Floyd and Vernita got into the car and drove off. The car excited Vernita. She snuggled close to Floyd, enjoying the moment they shared in his new gift.

"You are very lucky to have parents with money. I wish I were the only child."

"Don't ever wish that. I miss not having a brother or sister."

"I can't see why. You can get almost anything you want."

"No, I can't, not anything."

"Then tell me, what else do you want?"

"I want to be loved… no, you're right. Forget what I just said."

"No, Floyd, what's wrong with you? Something's wrong."

Floyd used his change-the-subject tactic. "You want to see a movie?"

"Yeah!"

He made a U-turn. "Let's go to the drive-in theater. I heard they have a good movie playing."

After they adjusted the speakers to the windows, Vernita questioned Floyd again about what was going on.

He replied, "Let's get in the backseat. We'll be more comfortable there. Do you want anything to eat?"

"No, but I would like something to drink." Vernita moved to the back seat when Floyd went to get the drinks. After taking a long sip of the soda, Vernita said, "Thanks for the Coke. Now, tell me what's going on with you."

Floyd put his arms around Vernita and kissed her. A deep, soft kiss.

Vernita pulled away. "Are you going to answer my question?"

"Maybe later."

He pulled her close again. Vernita returned his passionate kisses. They slid down onto the back seat of the car. They smiled at each other in the moonlight as they undressed one another, kissing gently and slowly. This caused their body temperatures to rise like mercury. The feature movie went unnoticed by the two lovebirds as they indulged in some *lusty* lovemaking.

They still lay tangled in each other's arms when Vernita said, "You knew that we were going to make love, didn't you?"

"No, but I bought the condom, just in case."

Although Vernita and Floyd were very much in love, she knew that the time had come for her to know the truth. Vernita had heard from Floyd's buddies that he used drugs, which devastated her. She confronted Floyd with the gossip during lunchtime, under their favorite oak at the far end of the school campus.

"Do I look like I would smoke pot?"

"No, but I don't know what a person looks like who does smoke pot."

"Look, baby, I love you. You mean everything to me."

"I love you too. But if you ever have a problem, please don't shut me out. You can tell me anything."

As juniors, Vernita and Carolyn had found that studying together for algebra tests raised their grades. This time, they met at Vernita's home. Vernita divulged what she knew about Floyd's drug habit. Feeling guilty, Carolyn shared with Vernita the news she had heard about Floyd and the night of the shooting. She disclosed that Floyd and his friends had smoked pot before the shooting. Vernita was furious.

Carolyn tried to calm her friend down. "Vernita, Floyd is mixed up. Floyd don't know what it is he wants to do. I think his problems are heavy, a lot having to do with his parents."

Tears trickled out of Vernita's eyes and down her cheeks. She asked, "But still, why can't he share it with me? Especially since we love one another."

"Now, Vernita, next time you see him, ask Floyd again about it. Maybe he's ready to come clean. But right now, let's take a break and dry those eyes."

That night, Floyd returned home early from the out-of-town basketball game. A riot had broken out outside the gym before game time, and the game was canceled. Floyd caught a ride home with a friend who lived near him and walked home from his friend's house.

Floyd entered the house and headed for his bedroom. He was surprised to hear some lusty moans and groans coming from his parents' bedroom. He knew that his father's car wasn't in the driveway, so he opened the door to the bedroom to see who was in there. To his amazement, Floyd saw his mother and Mrs. Williams naked in bed.

Seeing him standing in the doorway, Mrs. Williams screamed, "Oh, my God, it's Floyd!"

"What? Floyd! Baby, let mama explain," his mother cried, immediately getting out of bed, throwing her robe over herself and rushing toward him. Floyd first pulled away from his mother, then pushed her to the floor and said, "Don't you touch me, bitch. How could you… both of you are sick. I got to get out of here. It's true what they say about you!" "Floyd, come back here."

Floyd ran out the door and sped off in his car.

Mrs. Davis immediately called Vernita. Vernita heard an odd tone in Mrs. Davis's voice.

"Mrs. Davis, what's wrong?"

"Oh, it's nothing. Floyd and I had a little misunderstanding. He ran out of the house before I got a chance to explain. Please call me the minute you hear from him."

"Okay! Is there anything I can do?"

"No, Vernita, just do me that favor."

"Okay, Mrs. Davis." She slowly replaced the receiver.

"What was that all about?" Carolyn asked.

"That was Mrs. Davis, wanting to know if Floyd was here. She said they had a little misunderstanding, but her voice made it sound more serious."

"Wait a minute… didn't Floyd have a game out of town tonight?"

"Yeah, but his mom said that he was home early."

"Something is definitely wrong here," Carolyn concluded.

"Well, I guess we'll have to wait for Floyd to find out what."

Meanwhile, Floyd was driving on the interstate, still shocked and enraged at what he had seen. Unaware that he was speeding when he took the exit, he lost control of the car. It crashed head-on against a light pole and killed him instantly.

Mrs. Davis received a call from the police station, informing her of her son's death. She dropped the phone. Mrs. Williams picked up the phone and identified herself as a friend of the family. After the police officer told Mrs. Williams the news, she hung up the phone.

Mrs. Davis screamed, "Oh, my God! My baby's gone!" Her voice matched her angry look. "You are the reason my baby is dead. I have killed my son 'cause of you!"

Mrs. Williams grabbed Mrs. Davis by the shoulders and calmed her down before calling the distraught lady's husband. When he arrived home he noticed the condition of the bedroom as soon as he entered.

"What the hell is going on here?"

Mrs. Williams had her arms around his wife, comforting her. Mrs. Davis was sobbing, so Mrs. Williams spoke out, "Floyd was killed in a car crash!"

He looked at his wife. "Tell me Mrs. Williams is lying!"

His wife looked up at him. "No, the police called, and they want y'all to come and make a positive identification of Floyd."

The next day, Vernita heard the news of Floyd's death. Vernita was heartbroken. Silence was her reaction.

They held Floyd's funeral in the high school gym. A church couldn't accommodate the many students who wanted to pay their last respects to such a popular and lovable young man.

Floyd's parents divorced a few months after the funeral. Vernita continued to mourn his loss for a very long time.

SEDUCEMENT

Vernita found comforting words from her aunt Susan, who had experienced life and had lots of stories to tell about her two semesters in college, even though college had been cut short by a wedding. Susan also shared that she and Harold were having marital problems.

One day, just before her first class, Vernita happened to witness her uncle Harold kissing a student before the girl ran into school. Uncle Harold should have been working at that time of day. Taken aback, Vernita confided in her cousin Melissa during lunchtime about the incident.

Melissa was also shocked to hear that news, wondering what the hell was going on. "Do you think he is having an affair with that girl? You know, I heard it through the grapevine that girl was dating a married man." Taking matters into her own hands, Vernita decided to confront the girl. Between classes, she spotted her going into the restroom. Following her in, she pushed the girl against the wall. Vernita acted surprised and said, "Oh, excuse me."

"Damn, why don't you watch where you're going!" Vernita repeated, "I said, excuse me!"

The girl's friend asked, "What's going on, Brenda?"

"She stepped on my feet, that's what!" replied the girl.

Vernita put her hands on her hips, stared straight at Brenda, and snapped, "If you want to make a big issue out of this, we can. This will give me a good excuse to whip your ass and send you crying on Harold's shoulders."

"What… what do you know about Harold?"

"You mean *uncle* Harold. That's right, he's my uncle." She walked up closer to the girl and pointed her finger. "And I'd better not catch you in that car again. Do I make myself clear?"

"I ride with whomever I please, bitch! Just who do you think you are?" Melissa entered the bathroom looking for Vernita and broke up the girls' argument. As she escorted Vernita out the door, Vernita threatened Brenda again.

In the hallway, Vernita turned her resentment toward her cousin. "Melissa, I wanted to kick her ass."

"What has gotten into you? Acting this way isn't going to bring Floyd back. You got to let it go." Melissa pulled Vernita's arm, steering her to a bench in the corner of the hall.

Vernita collapsed onto the seat. She looked into her cousin's face as if she really expected the answer to her question. "Melissa, why did Floyd have to die? God knows. I ask Him every night, why did He have to take him away from me?"

"No, Vernita, there is no answer to death. But one thing's for sure, you're here. I know Floyd wouldn't want you to mourn him in this way. Those memories you shared with him will always be with you. Don't let his death destroy you."

Weeks later, Susan offered to drive Vernita to Carolyn's party. Susan showed up early and asked Vernita if she minded hanging out with her for a while. She promised to get her to the party on time. Vernita agreed, and Susan drove straight to a night club.

As they parked near the club, Vernita asked, "What are we doing here?"

"You can get out. It's too early for a crowd to be here yet. Besides, you're with me. Just let me do the talking."

Vernita shook her head at the same time as she peered out of the car at the neon lights surrounding the building. "I have never been to a club before. Mom would kill me if she knew where I was."

"Oh, please don't you dare tell Bertha," Susan demanded.

Vernita gave a quick, nervous laugh. "Oh, I won't…. This place is small," she observed.

"Yeah, but it be jumping, with people standing outside and along the walls."

After one drink, they went to another club. There they met some guys who offered to buy them drinks. Susan ordered a rum and Coke, while Vernita ordered a straight Coke.

"Come on, baby, I know you want more than a Coke," one of the guys teased.

"My girlfriend don't drink. Get the lady what she wants. Be a gentleman and don't push her."

"Okay, but before the night is over, she'll be drinking something heavy," the guy insisted. "What's your name?" he asked Vernita.

Susan jumped in and replied, "Her name is Vicky and mine's Lisa."

Vernita gave her aunt a squinty look when she heard the phony names. She asked, "What's y'all names?"

"This is Charles and I'm Mike. Vicky, would you like to dance?"

Susan urged, "Go ahead, Vicky."

"Sure," she said with a shrug.

Susan flirted with Charles while Vernita danced with Mike. Minutes before the club closed, Vernita looked at the time and wondered what her mom would say.

Mike saw her glance at her watch. He said, "I know where there's another club that's still open. Y'all wanna check it out?"

"That's cool with me," Susan said, getting up.

"Bu...but..." Vernita stuttered.

"Girl, don't worry," whispered Susan. "I got it under control."

Vernita announced, "I need to go to the restroom. Excuse me, Lisa, could you show me to the restroom?"

Outside of earshot of the guys, Vernita practically jumped on her aunt. "What do you think you're doing? We don't know these guys."

"Relax, Vernita, I'll leave my car parked and we'll ride with them. They won't do anything to us as long as we stick together."

Vernita was furious with her aunt but, at the same time, hoped everything would work out.

They returned to the table. "We decided to ride with you guys. That's if it's all right with y'all. But I need to park my car somewhere else."

Charles held the door open for them. "That's fine. Follow me, and I'll show you where you can park your car."

"What about Mike?" asked Vernita.

"He's with me. He'll be along in a minute."

"I don't like the sound of this," Vernita whispered in her aunt's ear.

Shush!" Susan said, frowning at Vernita.

Susan and Vernita walked to the car. While waiting for the guys to pull off and lead the way, Vernita voiced her concerns.

"I don't won't to go to another club, I want to go home."

"We're going home. They just want to party. Besides, we don't have to spend no money."

"I don't have any money anyway," Vernita reminded her.

"Right, and you don't need any. We are going to have fun. Didn't you notice that I didn't finish my drink? Honey, I knows what I'm doing. Relax, I'm not going to let anything happen to you."

When they arrived where Susan was to park her car, Charles strutted over and whispered something in Susan's ear. Susan told Vernita to get into the guy's car. Hesitating at first, Vernita got into the car with Mike, who offered her a beer.

"I told you that I don't drink." "Well, baby, I'm sorry."

Susan and Charles joined them after a couple long minutes. In the front seat, they soon were hugging, kissing, and whispering in each other's ears. Mike tried to make his move.

Vernita recoiled into her corner of the backseat and said in a loud voice, "Don't touch me."

Mike put up both hands in surrender. "Girl, I ain't going to bite. I just want to sit close, so I can talk with you."

"I can hear you clearly from here."

"Vernita, Charles and I are going to my car," Susan announced.

"What about me?" Vernita asked.

"I'm not going anywhere," Susan assured her.

"Wait a minute, Susan," Vernita yelled, managing to keep up the pretense even in her mounting anger.

"What do you want with me?" Susan asked, getting a little upset at her niece.

Mike explained, "You might as well relax. Your girlfriend and my boy are going to take care of business."

As soon as the car door closed, Mike moved himself against Vernita, planting a long kiss on her lips while his hands groped her breasts.

She struggled to push him away. "Listen, you and I are not going to be hitting it off. I'm too young for you. I'm only sixteen—and you're married. I can see the ring print around your finger."

Mike sat back a bit. "So what if I'm married. I still want to be with you. I like what I see and I want to be with you," he repeated.

"What about your wife? Please, Mike, if you care for me, you'll just take me home. Listen, we lied about our names. My name is Vernita Cleveland. I'm in high school. I'm supposed to be at my girlfriend's house, but my aunt asked me to hang out with her. Please, if you have any children, think about them someday being in my situation. Please, don't force me to have sex with you. Please."

Mike gently grabbed Vernita and held her in his arms. "Ahh, you're right, I am married. And I must tell you that your aunt won't be back for you. I'll take you home, but don't ever let your aunt talk you into hanging out with her again. 'cause if I was a maniac, I'd rape you. But I'm not, so I'll take you home."

Vernita felt her body relax as he spoke and then released her. She gushed, "Oh, thank you so much. You'll never know how much I appreciate this."

Mike drove Vernita home. Bertha was waiting up for her. She was furious at her daughter until Vernita explained what had happened. Bertha confronted her sister the next day and warned her never to get her daughter into that type of situation again.

DECEPTION

Lee, Martha's seventeen-year-old son, heard the news from his mother about his cousin. He called Vernita and asked to meet her in private at her house. She agreed to do so. When Lee arrived, Vernita ran to her cousin, hugging him as they went outside to the back porch. She dusted off the straight chairs with a towel before they sat to discuss her awful night.

"Vernita, I couldn't believe it when mama told me what happened. What has gotten into aunt Susan? I told Harold about what happened with your run-in at school with Brenda. And I cursed him out because of aunt Susan. I even promised him that I wasn't going to tell her about him sleeping around with all those girls at our school, but now…. God works in mysterious ways. You could have gotten raped or killed."

"Lee, I couldn't believe it myself! She changed right before my eyes. She didn't care about me. I didn't care if she wanted to hook up with that guy, but I thought that she would have taken me home. Huh! She dumped me out and ran off with that guy. What makes it so bad, she didn't even know him. They had just met. She gave them phony names. You just wouldn't believe what I went through. I broke down and told Mike… he's the one… you know… I told him the truth about us. He listened and brought me home, advising me not to hang out with aunt Susan again."

Lee and Vernita changed the topic of their conversation when Bro and Marilyn dropped by Bertha's house. Lee, Vernita, and Bertha wanted to know when they were getting married.

Bro answered, "Man, I don't know. I just decided to introduce her to the family." Feeling the tension, Bro asked, "What's going on, anyway?"

Reluctant to reveal what was going on with Vernita, because they all knew that Bro had a bad temper and didn't want him to get involved, the family continued to question the couple about their wedding plans. Lee, who worked part-time for Bro's construction company after school and on Saturdays, talked with him about plans to build a house, while Marilyn mingled with the other family members who were eager to get to know her.

Vernita noticed the tension between Bro and Lee. She cornered her cousin and asked, "What's going on between you and uncle Bro?"

"Nothing, he was just complaining about me not showing up for work." Then Lee came clean. "Vernita, I want you to meet my girlfriend."

"You got a girlfriend? Tell me who she is. I haven't seen you talking to anyone at school."

"She doesn't go to our school. I'm going to take you by her house one day."

A couple days later, Lee picked up Vernita and drove her to his girlfriend's house. Vernita was shocked. The "girl" was an older woman— much older than Lee. He introduced Vernita to his girlfriend, Anita. Although inwardly disappointed, Vernita was polite and nonjudgmental. She didn't mention her disapproval to Lee. Lee was happy and Vernita could see their affection for one another.

Within a few months, three emotional explosions hit the family. Bro married a woman the family never met, Rita Moore, who was pregnant with his child. Lee introduced Anita to the family. The family, at first, didn't know that Lee's girlfriend was also Bro's former lover. When Grandma Willie Mae found out that Bro and Lee both were involved with Anita, she couldn't contain herself. She blasted Lee for going with his uncle's woman and Bro for marrying a woman the family didn't know. In spite of the family warnings, Lee married Anita. He was not very concerned that the attractive woman had three kids, ranging in age from two through four.

Glad at the prospect of being away from the family's emotional turmoil, Vernita went off to college.

LOVE CONNECTION

Bertha refused to allow her sons, Will Jr. and Allen, to work with her brother Bro in his construction business. After what happened to Lee, she felt he was not the right role model for them. She felt justified in her decision, as she was still separated from Will and receiving child support for them. She would rather her sons seek employment with another company, which she stressed to her sons and Bro.

During their family meetings, she expressed the importance of education to her children. She told them about the dangers of peer pressure and encouraged them to seek her support whenever they were troubled. Her lectures stemmed from the recognition that the lack of parental guidance rose rapidly during this era of two-income families and, oftentimes, maternally-headed black households. She was aware that drugs and alcohol contributed to the lack of initiative among youth. In such a culture, it became all too common for teenagers to kill each other, while the number of teenage mothers increased at an alarming rate.

Vernita loved college life. Faye, her roommate, became a close friend. They had a lot in common, part of that being a lot of time spent together in joint tutoring sessions for their chemistry class.

Mr. Washington, a professor at the college, admired Vernita, although secretly, more than was appropriate. One day, unaware of his strong feelings for her, she sought his help for a problem she had in chemistry class. He offered to tutor her at the library, and Vernita was eager to accept.

One afternoon after their tutoring session, Faye asked, "Vernita, would you like to check out this new club?"

"I don't know, all this studying has me whipped."

"We're always studying. It's time for us to relax."

"Okay, I'll go."

"Good. I knew I could talk you into it!"

They arrived at the club after nine o'clock and seated themselves at a table. Soon the place was packed. Sitting at the bar was Mr. Washington. Faye spotted him through the crowd and saw that he kept looking toward them.

"Vernita, there's Mr. Washington, sitting at the bar!"

"Where?" she asked, her eyes scanning the bar stools.

Faye didn't want to point, even if the place was crowded. "He's over there, at the right end of the bar."

"Oh. Now, I see him."

Faye was checking her lipstick. She suggested, "We ought to go and speak with him."

Vernita agreed. "Yeah, we could do that."

They went to the bar and said hello to Mr. Washington. The DJ played Vernita's song. She tuned in to it and began to move with the rhythm.

Mr. Washington noticed Vernita's response to the song. "Vernita, would you like to dance?"

"Oh, no, that's all right."

"Oh, I see. You don't want to dance with your professor."

"No, I didn't mean it like that."

"So, let's dance."

In fact, they danced to several songs. Afterward, he escorted Vernita to the table, and complimented her dancing and her appearance. After sitting a couple minutes, he said goodnight to them and left the club.

Vernita and Faye immediately began to talk about him. Vernita revealed, "I didn't know that Mr. Washington could dance. He said he likes to dance. He asked me if we came here often. I told him this was my first time."

Faye grinned and gave her friend's arm a slight push. "Girl, Mr. Washington has a thing for you."

"Oh, Faye, please don't start in on me."

"I'm serious. You'll see, mark my word on this one."

Mr. Washington and Vernita became friends. He even offered for her to call him by his first name, Julian. After that semester, though, they didn't see much of each another. One night, Vernita and Faye bumped into him at a club. He offered the girls a ride home. Faye wasn't ready to leave, but Vernita accepted the ride. On the way home, Julian suggested they go to another club or to his place to watch television or listen to music.

"Well, we could go to your place until Faye gets home."

"Sounds good to me," he said with a lustful smile.

Entering his home, Vernita noted the size of the rooms as she walked around, looking at his paintings and knickknacks. "This is a big house. You live here by yourself?" she asked.

"Yep, I sure do."

"I don't mean to pry, but is there a Mrs. Washington?"

"No, I'm divorced. I've been divorced two years now."

Pointing to a picture of a child, Vernita asked, "Who is this?"

"That's my nephew, my sister's little boy. I don't have any children. My wife had female problems, so we didn't have any children," he explained.

"I'm sorry to hear that."

"Don't be. It just wasn't meant to be."

They continued their conversation, learning more about one another as the evening lingered on. Vernita revealed her past relationship with Floyd, expressing her fears of getting involved with anyone else.

Julian comforted her, which led to passionate kissing. While kissing her, he expressed his desire for her. He promised not to hurt or pursue her if the feeling wasn't mutual. Vernita had no objections and allowed him to pursue his desire for her. They fondled each other, kissing one another in all the right places. Their clothing melted off, and the kissing and fondling got deeper. With her permission, Julian introduced Vernita to oral sex by placing his lips and tongue on, between, and around her clitoris, licking and tonguing it gently. To Vernita, his mouth looked like a glazed doughnut when he finally raised his head from her now sopping, wet vagina. She urged him onto her. He penetrated her, causing her to squeal with pleasure.

Meanwhile, Faye had returned home, and there was no sign of Vernita. She left to check with classmates to see whether or not they had seen Vernita. No one had. Faye returned to their dorm room, hoping that nothing bad had happened to Vernita.

Vernita wobbled in at six o'clock the next morning. Faye, worried to death about her roommate and friend, asked, "Where have you been?"

"Girl, you ain't going to believe what happened to me." "Try me," said Faye, crossing her arms.

Vernita gently sat on her bed. "I can't believe it myself. You were right about Julian. He's in love with me."

"Girl, what have you been smoking?"

"No, it's true. I'm serious. We admitted and showed each other our feelings towards one another last night. I spent the night in bed with him."

"Wait a minute. No—are sure about this? He could be married."

"Believe me, he's not. He's divorced. I saw the papers. He showed them to me while we ate breakfast."

"My Lord, girlfriend, he's a professor!"

"I know, we talked about that. We're going to work that out. He managed to sneak me back on campus without anyone seeing us."

"Vernita, I don't know about this. He's much too old for you. He's ten, maybe fifteen, years older."

"Okay, so the man is ten years older than me," Vernita said, getting irritated with her friend's barrage of questions. "So what? That still doesn't change how we feel about one another. Can't you be happy for me and wish me well in this relationship?"

"Yeah, but I still can't believe it…. You and Mr. Washington," Faye said, smiling.

THE REUNION;
MID-EIGHTIES

◆

Thomas Turner returned to Miami, Florida with his wife, Ella, who was terminally ill with cancer. The doctors told him that she only had six months to live.

One afternoon, Bertha got a strange phone call. Lisa ran to the phone and said, "Hello."

"Bertha, is that you?"

"No, this is her daughter, Lisa." "Hi, this is Papa."

"Papa who?"

"I'm your granddaddy, your mother's father. Is your mama at home?"

"Yeah," she answered, and without covering the mouthpiece she yelled out, "Mom, the telephone—it's your daddy."

Bertha stopped knitting and walking over to the phone, said, "What? Lisa Ann, don't be lying to me. Now, who is it?"

"Mom, I ain't kidding you. The man said 'it's Papa,' then I said, 'Papa who?' then he said, 'your granddaddy."

"Girl, give me this phone…. Hello?"

"Bertha, it's me, your daddy."

"Dad! Well, I'll be…."

Bertha was glad to hear from her father. She settled into a nearby easy chair. Thirty years had passed since she last heard from him. He told her he was home for good. He also said he was in good health, but his wife had cancer. He asked about the rest of the family, including Willie Mae. At the end of the phone call, Bertha invited Thomas to visit them anytime.

Bertha received yet another surprise. Vernita and her handsome, older boyfriend Julian Washington came home to visit. When most of the family was gathered, they informed everyone of their engagement.

Bertha was saddened, not because of their engagement, but because of the timing and Julian's age. She had hoped that Vernita would marry a man her own age and *after* she finished college. But if her daughter would decide to marry while she was in college, she would give her blessings, providing she would continue her education. Bertha and Vernita had a private talk. Vernita assured her mother that she would finish college. And that she really loved Julian. Bertha could see they were deeply in love, and she gave Vernita her blessings.

A couple months later, Vernita and Julian married. They had a simple wedding at Bertha's home, inviting only a few friends and some family members, including Bertha's father and Will, who proudly gave his daughter away.

Everyone welcomed Thomas's return back home—except Henry. The family held a soul food buffet dinner for Thomas. They gathered in the living room, drinking punch with each family member in turn chatting with Thomas. After waiting and watching patiently, Henry finally raised up from the couch and slowly, with a pained frown, drew near his father.

In a low voice, Henry said, "Dad, how could you show up here after the hell you put this family through?"

Thomas pointed his pipe in Vernita's direction. "Son, that's my granddaughter getting married. Besides, I've changed. I'm not the man you knew thirty years ago."

"Well, you may fool them but you don't fool me. As far as I'm concerned, you're dead." Henry turned and went to the kitchen. The screen door slammed.

Thomas' eyes filled with tears. He had been unaware that his son harbored so much anger toward him. He had to walk off and wipe his face with his handkerchief before he could continue mingling with the rest of his family and friends.

Three months later, Thomas's wife died. He started visiting his children and grandchildren frequently, forming close relationships with them. He also wanted to be friends with his ex-wife, Willie Mae. That was asking a lot though, because she couldn't forget the past.

REVENGE

During spring break of her senior year, Lisa Ann visited her sister in Atlanta, Georgia. As she and Vernita were walking through the mall, Lisa Ann revealed that she was pregnant. Vernita was shocked and had to sit on the nearest bench. She soon recovered enough to question her sister about the circumstances.

"How could you let this happen? Didn't it ever cross your mind to use some protection or just wait? My God, you are too young to be a mother."

"I know, that's why I'm here. I want to get an abortion."

"An abortion! Does mother know that you're pregnant?"

"No! And my boyfriend gave me the money for the abortion. Please, Sis, I need your help."

Reluctantly, Vernita arranged for her sister to see a doctor. On the day of the abortion, a confused and disappointed Vernita waited in the lobby of the doctor's office, pacing the floor and praying. Lisa Ann approached from behind and touched her shoulder.

Vernita turned and caught her in a hug. "Thank God, you're all right."

Lisa Ann held her sister's hands. She said, "Yeah, I'm fine… and still pregnant. They couldn't do it. I'm four months' pregnant. They don't give abortions this far into a pregnancy."

She sank back into Vernita's enfolding arms and soothing words. "Baby, I'm sorry. It just isn't God's will to abort this baby."

Lisa Ann went home and told her boyfriend, Freddie Parker, what had happened. Freddie, a young black man who worked hard to maintain his muscular yet small physique, accepted his money back, happy that Lisa Ann didn't get the abortion.

Lisa Ann finally told her mother about her condition and of the reason for her visit to Vernita. Bertha was also glad that Lisa didn't abort the baby. Freddie assured Bertha that he would take full responsibility of providing for his child. He even offered to marry Lisa Ann, but after some thought and family consultations, Lisa Ann couldn't see being a young bride and a mother too. She insisted on finishing school first.

Freddie started selling drugs and managed to keep his criminal activity a secret from Lisa Ann. She did question him about the money. He claimed that he had a part-time job, which he wouldn't name.

One evening, Freddie visited Lisa Ann, acting very preoccupied. Lisa Ann asked him about his odd behavior. He claimed that he had a problem involving work. Freddie left early, saying he was exhausted.

From a nearby telephone booth, he called his friend Folly about the meeting with Ace, a drug dealer. Folly said to meet him at a barn-style, brown house located a few miles south of town. Freddie followed Folly's directions and drove until he spotted a house in the middle of a wooded area. Nothing for miles—if anything happened, no one would be able to hear shots or cries for help. Nevertheless, he drove down the long narrow dirt road leading to the house. Several cars were parked in front. He hesitated for a moment and then slowly got out of his car. A burly biker type spotted him from the front door entrance of the house and waved him in.

It turned out to be an unpleasant meeting. The drug dealer was mad, and armed. Ace's gang members slouched in every chair in the room, and some were standing, ready to do his bidding.

Freddie said as casually as he could, "Hey, bro, what's up? Folly here?"

Ace, dressed down to only one heavy gold chain necklace, had a slight grin on his face as he walked toward Freddie. He reached out and grabbed his hand to give him a welcome handshake. He squeezed Freddie's hand tightly, dropping Freddie to his knees. "Don't play me, Freddie boy," Ace snarled. "You know what's up. You've been trying to run a scam. You've been taking money off the top."

"Man, I paid you for the smoke."

"Yeah, but I heard you've been splitting my shit. Folks be complaining about how I do business. You know what happens to people who try to shit Ace."

"Ace, let me explain! Please… man, let me explain! I've got a baby on the way. My lady is due any day now. Please don't do this. If you don't give a damn about me, think about my lady and child."

"Yeah, I'm going to think about your lady and child, all right. Boys, teach him Lesson Three."

A couple minutes later, cars pulled up outside. It was Folly and his boys. But they were too late—Ace's boys had beaten Freddie bad out in front of the house, and left him lying in the dirt and blood. The place was abandoned.

Folly jumped out of the car and rushed to aid his friend. "Freddie, hang in there. Lisa Ann and the baby need you. Y'all call for an ambulance," Freddie directed one of the guys.

Meanwhile, Lisa Ann was stretched across her bed. She was still confused about the way Freddie had acted when he was over earlier. The phone rang.

"Lisa Ann?"

"Yes. Who's this?"

"This is Folly. I'm in the emergency room at the hospital. Freddie's been hurt."

"What! Oh, no! What do you mean he's been hurt?"

"Now don't you worry, he's gonna be all right. But you need to be here."

"I'm on my way." She hung up the phone and called out, "Mom!"

"Baby, what's the matter? Are you in pain?" Bertha said as she appeared at the bedroom door.

"No, it's Freddie. I've got to go to the hospital. He's been hurt."

"Hurt! Was he in an accident?"

"I don't know. Folly just called from the emergency room and said that Freddie's been hurt."

Bertha drove Vernita to the hospital. When they entered the lobby, they saw many of Freddie's family members and friends. Freddie's mother hugged both Lisa and Bertha then began crying.

Lisa Ann asked Folly, "What's going on with Freddie?"

"The doctors are with him now. We haven't heard anything."

"Folly, you called me, what happened?"

"I don't know what happened. I went to meet Freddie at our hangout. And found him lying in the dirt all bloody."

"Oh, my God, was he shot?"

"No, someone beat him bad. Slashed his face, legs and arms."

Lisa Ann walked away from Folly. She rushed toward the emergency room, screaming as loud as he could, "Freddie, Freddie!"

A nurse and a police officer removed her from the area and tried to calm her down. But Lisa Ann fell to the floor, clutching her abdomen and crying in pain. The nurse ran for help. Soon a doctor and the nurse came and took

Lisa Ann to the emergency room. Now Freddie's parents and Bertha were also concerned about Lisa's and the unborn child's conditions.

The doctor told the concerned parents that Lisa had gone into labor. Moments later, they get a report about Freddie's condition. The doctor assured the family that he would recover.

Freddie's mother asked, "When can we see him?"

The doctor answered, "They are moving him to a room now. Your son has a fractured rib, so he's in pain."

Mrs. Teresa left to see her son while Bertha waited for some news about her daughter's condition. Hours later, the doctor informed Bertha that her daughter had given birth to a girl, who weighed only one and a half pounds. She was so tiny that the doctor was not sure if she would survive. He said that Lisa Ann would be okay. He then escorted the nervous mother to her daughter's room.

"Mom, it's a girl!" Lisa Ann said, smiling.

"Yeah, mama knows."

"How's Freddie doing?"

"He's fine. The doctor says that he'll be up and about in no time."

Hearing the news about Lisa Ann relieved Freddie. Although he was in pain, the news that he was a father delighted him. Two days later, the baby died. Devastated, Lisa blamed herself for the child's death. When Freddie found out, he blamed his unfortunate incident on causing Lisa's premature labor.

He wanted revenge. He told Folly about his plans to get Ace. Folly refused to get involved and insisted that Freddie drop the issue. Concerned for his friend, Folly told Freddie's mother about her son's intentions. She reacted by sending Freddie away to live with distant relatives.

Lisa Ann grieved for months about the death of her child. Bertha assured her daughter that, in time, the emotional wounds would heal.

VICTIM

Vernita, Julian, and their children went home to Alabama to visit Bertha. Lisa Ann confided in Vernita about losing her baby. Though Lisa Ann had initially considered abortion, she had bonded closely with the unborn child later in her pregnancy. She told Vernita she felt that God punished her for considering an abortion.

Vernita assured her that it wasn't her fault. "Death happens. There's nothing we can do to prevent it. Besides, you're too young to be a mother. Now, you can continue school and, later, enjoy a wonderful home and life with someone you love."

Vernita's grandfather took ill during their visit. The doctors diagnosed him as having lung cancer. He had to undergo radiation to treat his condition. As time progressed, Thomas became weaker and weaker.

To relieve some of the stress, Vernita and Julian decided to go to a club. She became reacquainted with an old girlfriend, Cynthia, who came by when she recognized Vernita. Vernita introduced her to Julian and invited her old friend and her companion to join them at their table.

They reminisced about mutual friends. Cynthia asked, "When was the last time you heard from Carolyn?"

"I haven't heard from her in a long time."

"You mean you haven't heard that she's strung out on crack?"

In an instant, Vernita's smile disappeared. "Crack? I can't believe that. Carolyn had it all going on. She comes from a well-to-do family. The last I heard, she attended college majoring in business management."

"I'm telling you, girlfriend is on that shit. And she's as skinny as a prune. I couldn't believe when I heard it either. The talk on the street is that home girl is into anything and everything, including prostitution, or "strawberrying" as they call the crack hoes. She lost her job and sold all her shit." Cynthia sat back and waited for a reaction.

"Wait a minute! Julian, Carolyn and I were the best of friends. Cynthia, you're lying. Are you sure we're talking about the same girl?" Vernita asked.

"Why would I lie about that? Check it out for yourself. She's in the rehab center. Well, it's nice seeing you again. Check out home girl before you split," Cynthia said as got up and left.

Vernita turned to her husband. "Julian, I can't believe this."

"Baby, I don't know about Carolyn, but Cynthia could be lying. She's something else herself. You can tell by her conversation that she is high," Julian added.

Vernita and Julian enjoyed their night out, mingling among their friends. Still, Vernita worried about Carolyn.

The next day, Vernita visited the rehabilitation center. Vernita inquired about Carolyn at the receptionist desk and confirmed that Carolyn indeed was a patient at the center. The atmosphere amazed her. She had never been to a rehab center before. She waited in the reception area. Patients approached her, asking for cigarettes and admiring her appearance, wondering if she was a doctor. The patients really looked bad. After arranging for Vernita to visit her friend, a nurse escorted her to the patients' visiting lounge. Moments later, Carolyn walked into the lounge escorted by one of the nurses. The sight of her shocked Vernita. Carolyn had lost a lot of weight, her hairline had receded, her lips were blistered, and dry facial skin dotted the front of her dark blue shirt.

"Carolyn, it's Vernita."

"Vernita, is that you?"

After embracing one another, the girls chatted about the past. Carolyn told Vernita the horrifying story of how she got hooked on crack cocaine. She even confessed that she had begun by smoking pot, sometimes with Floyd, Vernita's high school sweetheart.

Carolyn said that she tried crack once and became addicted. Her story was the same as the one Cynthia had told her, and more. She explained that she ended up in the rehab center after her family became aware of her addiction.

"Vernita," she continued. "At first I was angry with my family for putting me in this place. But now I'm glad. There is no cure. I'll always be a victim. I'll have to take it one day at a time. And pray to God to give me the strength and courage to see me through. I have to thank him daily for my life."

Vernita was glad that she went to visit Carolyn. She thanked God for protecting her from also becoming a victim of drugs. She told Julian about it. They discussed the impact of crack and how it affected people—lost jobs, souls, and destroyed families. The young and old were victims of this poison, as it had nearly wiped out a whole generation of youth and showed no signs of letting up.

Vernita chatted with Grandfather Thomas before leaving town. He told her how proud he was of her and the family, and that he loved them. Silently, she forgave him for not giving a thought to the fact that he was never there for her when she was growing up. The tone of his voice implied that he might not be able to say it again.

LAST REQUEST

After Lisa Ann went off to college, Freddie came home and married a girl he had met during his isolation. Thomas became too ill to be alone and moved in with Bertha. Martha aided Bertha with Thomas's care. Henry stopped over occasionally, but only to see his mother, Willie Mae. He still refused to have anything to do with his father.

Willie Mae confronted Henry about his attitude and advised him to pray and ask God to give him the strength to forgive his father, who was dying. Henry, however, even after hearing his mother's plea, could not find it in his heart to forgive his father.

Thomas died within the week. All of his family attended the funeral except Henry. He remained at home.

After the funeral, Willie Mae visited with her son. "I know your dad was dead to you years ago. But today, we put him in his resting place. Son, please find it in your heart to forgive him someday. Your dad told me to tell you before he died that he still loved you and that he always will. He understood why you kept your distance, and hoped that you would, one day, forgive him."

Bertha's neighbor's son told her one day about a kid who brought a gun to school and threatened to shoot a classmate. A gang member had bullied the neighbor's son and he had carried the gun to school for protection.

School let out early that day because of the incident. Bertha told Willie Mae about the gun-totin' student. They couldn't believe that things had gotten so bad that it wasn't even safe in school. After hearing this frightening news, Bertha called Vernita so she could chit-chat with her grandchildren.

Afterward, while talking with her mother, Vernita disclosed about her upcoming doctor's appointment and scheduled mammogram. Bertha sensed from the tone of her daughter's voice that Vernita feared having this examination. She reassured her daughter that everything would be all right and that she would say a prayer for her.

Vernita had her first mammogram and, unfortunately, the results were abnormal. The doctor requested more testing. She revealed the test results to her family and asked the older relatives if the family had any history of breast cancer. She found out that no one in the present generations had ever had the disease.

The doctor recommended that Vernita have a biopsy, as a biopsy was the only way to determine if the lump was cancerous. Julian was devastated, though outwardly, he tried to stay calm. He knew that whatever happened, Vernita would need his support. Vernita checked into the hospital a day before the surgery for out patient pre-op examination procedures. Another lump was discovered with that examination.

This revelation made Vernita a nervous wreck. She tried not to lose control, but the thought of losing one of her breasts was devastating. She stood in front of the mirror and tried to imagine how she would look with only one breast, and she prayed to God to save her breast.

Julian saw his emotional wife become more and more hysterical as the time for surgery drew nearer. He assured her that everything would work out. Vernita read her Bible constantly.

As he drove Vernita to the hospital, Julian could see the troubled look on her face. "Are you okay?"

"I'm fine," was her reply.

Upon arriving at the hospital, the doctor wasted no time in prepping Vernita for surgery. Julian stayed at Vernita's bedside, tenderly wiping the tears from her eyes, assuring her that everything would be fine and encouraging her to be strong.

The surgery lasted for more than three hours. When Vernita was wheeled into her room, Julian was there, wide awake, sitting in a chair next to the bed. The doctors had good news—the lumps were benign.

Tears flooded Vernita's face. Julian also cried and embraced his wife, thanking God.

That Sunday the Washingtons attended church. They wanted to thank God properly. A mixed crowd, representing many races, filled the church. The guest speaker was a white minister. During the service, Reverend Bryant introduced a young black teenager named Ellis Howard so he could recite his presentation. Ellis had also spoken at the previous service. Ellis' presentation touched the hearts of the congregation, young and old. He shared with everybody his previous experiences: being a gang member, shoplifting, and using and selling drugs. He preached to the congregation about the circumstances that caused him to succumb to society's evils—a lack of parental guidance a bad relationship with his stepfather, and peer pressure.

And, although he still related poorly with his stepfather, he emphasized his love for his mother, which inspired him to prevail. Getting caught shoplifting caused him to change. His mother picked him up from the police station and didn't say anything except to ask if he was okay.

He spoke of the impact of parental understanding, and that their support is what teenagers look for, whether they know it or not. He reminded the teenagers in attendance of the effect of money: easy come, easy go. And the importance of parents maintaining respect for themselves and their children by not cursing, drinking, or smoking crack and marijuana. He preached that teenagers need mentors and moral support in their homes and communities.

The people attending worship responded to Ellis's speech with loud, long clapping and shouts of amen. When the applause stopped, Reverend Bryant introduced Ellis's mother to the congregation. The Washington family enjoyed the service immensely. It gave them a message that they would treasure for life.

A NEW FRIEND

After the church service, some parishioners gathered in front of the church. Vernita and her family introduced themselves to the Howards and congratulated Ellis on his presentation.

Vernita's son JW, repeated what his mother had said. "That was a nice speech."

Ellis answered, "Thanks. Hey, JW, come join our chorus."

JW gave a shy smile and said, "Man, I can't sing. But I'm glad to hear that you joined the church. I heard that you got baptized too."

"I did. Where was you last Sunday?"

"My mother took ill and had to have an operation, but she's better now."

"Hey, man, good luck," Ellis offered as he followed his family to their car.

That evening, JW and Vernita discussed Ellis. "Mom, Ellis is in some of my classes. He's one of the boys I told you about that sold drugs at our school."

"Well, JW, the boy has decided to change his life. That was a wonderful speech. I wish more of our young people would change. It looks like there's some hope for young Ellis. I hope he stays in church."

"Mom, can I be friends with him now that he's not hanging out with that gang? Can Ellis come over sometimes?" JW asked.

"Sure, I don't see why not. He seems like a fine young man. But remember, you can only have company when your daddy and I are home."

JW whined, "Mom, I know."

"I'm just reminding you," Vernita added.

Meanwhile, Vernita's daughter Andrea wanted to attend the prom.

Knowing how protective her father was, she asked her mother first. In her sweetest voice, she said, "Mom, I want to go to the prom." "When is it?" Vernita asked.

"Next month. Can I go?"

"Who are you going with? I haven't seen anyone special hanging around here."

Andrea, now in an exasperated tone of voice, said, "Mom, I'm going with Troy Williams."

"Okay, but we've got to meet this young man. And we have to go shopping. Have you asked your daddy?"

"No, I wanted to tell you first. Dad's always saying that he has to think about it. But when JW asks him something, it's always okay."

"Well, I'll tell your daddy about the prom. 'cause you're right. If he had his way, there would be no prom. But don't worry, you're going to the prom."

Vernita waited for the right moment to talk with Julian about the prom. Julian asked, "Who is she going to the prom with?"

"A young man named Troy Williams."

"I'm going to have to meet Troy before I give my okay. We're going to have a long man-to-man talk before he takes my daughter anywhere. I might even show him my piece, so he won't get no ideas about messing around with my baby."

"Your gun? You can't be serious!"

Vernita said, astonished. "Huh! You want to bet?"

Vernita and Andrea were out shopping when Troy unexpectedly came over. Julian escorted him to the family room and had a long conversation with him. Andrea was afraid Troy would change his mind once her father had finished grilling him. The opposite happened, though; Troy admired Julian and respected his wishes.

After the prom, Andrea and Troy started dating more steadily. Vernita was concerned about her daughter growing up too fast. She decided to have a woman-to-woman talk with Andrea. After all, they did have an open, honest, and close mother-to-daughter relationship. Vernita devoted a lot of time bonding with her family. She was friendly but still had their respect and trust, even after she disciplined them. She taught her children how to survive and deal with peer pressure.

Vernita arranged for Andrea to see a gynecologist to have her first Pap smear test. She discussed the procedures and what to expect. And although she was very nervous, Andrea agreed to go. They arrived at the doctor's office and, while waiting her turn, Andrea was questioned by the nurse receptionist. The questioning amazed the young lady. Especially when the receptionist asked if she was pregnant. Andrea then told the receptionist that this was her first visit to a gynecologist and that her mother had accompanied her.

The startled receptionist said to Vernita, "Ma'am, we have to ask all the patients these questions." She said to Vernita, "You are a good mother."

"Thank you," Vernita replied.

Mother and daughter returned to their seats in the waiting area.

Vernita whispered, "Mom, why did she say that?"

"Andrea, many parents don't involve themselves with taking their daughter to have a Pap test. But I love you and I want the best for you. This is an important step in becoming a woman."

"Mom, I'm scared."

"It scared me when I had my first one, too. And I was alone. Remember what I told you, just relax and everything will be all right."

The doctor finally called Andrea to his office. Vernita patiently waited in the reception area. After thirty minutes, the doctor called for Vernita to join them.

"Your daughter wanted you to know about her examination. Everything is fine. We talked about the different sexual diseases, especially AIDS, a fatal disease. I told her never to have sex without examining the guy's penis thoroughly. I couldn't finish the examination because it became uncomfortable for her to continue. So I suggested that she start using tampons. I will see her again, hopefully, in a few months. I'm also going to give her some mild birth control pills for cramps."

Vernita and Andrea waited in the lounge area until the prescription was ready.

"Mom, it hurt. I thought I was going to die when he stuck his hand in me. And it was embarrassing having my legs in those stirrups and my legs wide open."

"Now, Andrea, it wasn't that bad. Obviously, you're still a virgin and that's why it felt so uncomfortable to you. If you start using tampons, it will be easier the next time."

"No, it won't. You never have to worry about my being anxious or curious about sex again."

They continued discussing the experience. Andrea let her mother know how much she appreciated her being there. No longer did she have the desire to rush into a sexual relationship.

Troy and Andrea continued to see one another as friends. Troy wanted a sexual relationship but Andrea wasn't interested. She concentrated on finishing high school with plans for college.

JW and Ellis became close friends. The Howards accepted an invitation to a barbecue at Vernita's home. Vernita watched as Julian and Ellis' father, Robert, talked with each other during the cookout. Julian shared the conversation with his wife later that evening.

"Vernita, Robert is very troubled. He thinks that he's going to be laid off his job. I tried to assure him to think positive, but he's so sure that he's next in line. Then he throws my job up in my face, saying that I don't have to worry 'cause I'm a school principal."

"Honey, all we can do is offer our support. Times are hard. We're in a depression, though our government says we're not. Jobs are tight. Lord knows I pray that you and I hold onto our jobs."

"Yeah, you're right. I told him that he ought to bring his family to our church. It helps me. But he claims he's too busy for that."

"Just keep at him. Maybe soon, he'll go. Ellis sure has changed and appears happy with himself. He sure is a positive influence for JW," Vernita added.

One day, JW bumped into Ellis after school. While walking home together, they were approached by two members of the Raiders Gang, who blocked their path. JW was wearing a popular Lakers starter jacket and the latest style Reebok sneakers. Ellis had forgotten to warn JW that the Raiders hung out in his neighborhood.

One of the young toughs said, "That's a bad jacket you're wearing." Ellis said, "Why don't y'all back off?"

"So look at what we have here, Reverend Ellis," they teased.

"Yeah, that's right," Ellis said.

"We just want to chat with your friend here, maybe teach him a few lessons. You do remember the lessons, don't you, Ellis?"

Ellis pleaded, "Leave him alone. Go pick on somebody else."

One of the guys said, "Fuck that! We want the jacket."

"Well, y'all aren't gonna get no jacket," Ellis stated.

JW said, "Here, take the jacket."

"See, my man, he has a lot of sense," the talkative gang member said. "You should take some lessons from him, Ellis my boy. You must have lost a screw."

"Let's go, man, we got the jacket," one of the quieter thugs urged.

The boys ran off with the jacket. Ellis was angry. He couldn't believe that he was once a part of a gang.

Ellis stated, "You didn't have to give them your jacket. I could have taken them out."

"It was only a jacket," replied JW. "Besides, no one got hurt. Remember, no violence. You're not like them anymore."

The boys had resumed walking, but Ellis headed for a bus bench and JW joined him.

"I never told you about the times I hung with the Raiders. Man, we did some heavy stuff. You know that teenager who got beaten and was hospitalized? I was there when it happened. He got beat over a jacket. We were all high on drugs," he added. "What really made me sick inside was when T raped that pretty schoolteacher, Mrs. Adams. I still hear in my dreams sometimes, that woman pleading for her life. She begged him not to kill her, but he held her down on the ground, with a pocket knife to her throat, and called her bitch while he raped her. He said he just wanted to scare her by running her car off the road. But then he demanded us to get out of the car and look out for the cops. We had to watch while he raped that woman."

JW said, "Man, how could you live with yourself and continue to hang out with those people? Especially after they raped the schoolteacher. Man, that's deep. I just can't believe that you would be a part of something like this."

Ellis continued, "We were sick. I smoked pot. I never tried crack because I was scared. I saw how it affected people. Women selling their food stamps and bodies for a hit of crack. This world is sick. I'm glad I got caught shoplifting, 'cause that's when my life changed."

JW sat in stunned silence.

Ellis said, "The teacher T raped had AIDS."

"What?" JW asked.

"Yap, I heard my parents talking about Mrs. Adams after she got raped. They said she left town because she didn't want to be raped again."

"No wonder she said that. So that means that T could have AIDS too."

JW and Ellis told their parents what happened with the Raiders. Everyone was relieved that they were unharmed.

ABUSE

One week after the jacket incident, Ellis came to school bruised up. JW asked his friend about the bruises. He claimed some Raiders gang members attacked him because his leaving the gang upset them and they wanted him back.

JW didn't believe his friend's story, so he confided in his parents, who admitted that Ellis' story could be true. JW, however, still had his doubts.

While playing basketball in JW's backyard, Ellis complimented JW on his loving family and his friendly neighborhood.

"I wished I could live in a mixed neighborhood," Ellis thought aloud.

JW picked up on the family issue and asked, "Don't your parents love each other?"

Ellis sounded more pitiful with each word. "I don't think so. My father doesn't care about us like your father cares about you. I know he don't love me."

JW questioned his friend. "Yes, he does. Why are you talking like this? What's the matter?"

"Just forget it, let's play ball. I was just kidding," Ellis said, as his mood instantly changed from depressed to happy.

It was Sunday and Robert Howard still refused to go to church with his wife and son.

"Dad, when are you going to go to church with us?" Ellis asked.

"Listen, boy, don't you start questioning me about religion. I'll go when I'm ready. Do I make myself clear? Besides, I pray at home. You and your mom can pray in the church," he explained.

"But still, it wouldn't hurt to go to church," Ellis insisted.

"Listen, you and your mom go," Robert said abruptly, ending the conversation.

Weeks later, Robert's job laid him off. Having no job to go to made Robert feel depressed and angry. The Howards household filled with tension every time church was mentioned. Ellis continued to ask his stepfather to attend church, but it was hopeless.

One day after school, Ellis was doing his homework. Robert had been drinking heavily. Ellis took a break from his schoolwork. He turned off the television—which his father was watching—and started to read his Bible. Robert grabbed Ellis, taking the Bible from his son's hand and tossing it onto the floor. Robert demanded the television be turned back on. Ellis did so and went back to his reading.

Robert watched a news report about the beating of an African-American man, Rodney King, by the police in Los Angeles, California. The beating occurred after the police officers had handcuffed Mr. King. Robert, in a rage, again snatched the Bible from his son. "Dammit, boy! I'm tired of you and your mama picking up this Bible. It isn't gonna help us. You see," he said, pointing to the television. "The white man is still in control. They're still beating us like they did in slavery. There isn't a God. Look—listen to the news. Tell me, where is your God?"

"Dad, I can only pray for this man. I don't have the answer, but I do have faith."

"Damn faith! I'll show you where faith will get you."

He grabbed Ellis and started beating him like he had stolen something from him. Moments later, JW knocked on the Howards' door. Ellis, crying and scared, didn't answer. Robert turned him loose and walked out the back door. JW heard the back door slam, so he went around the back and saw Ellis's father driving away.

JW found his friend lying on the floor, unable to move. He immediately telephoned his mother. Vernita answered and informed Julian, who had just walked in the door, "That was JW on the phone. He says that Mr. Howard beat Ellis bad."

"What? Robert better not have laid his hands on my boy."

"Honey, let's go. I'm sure JW is fine. It's Ellis's well-being that concerns me."

Vernita and Julian soon arrived at the Howards' house.

"What happened?" they asked in unison.

"Mom! Dad! Mr. Howard jumped on Ellis."

"Oh, my God, Julian, this boy is messed up… call 911!"

"How could he do this? I could—"

Vernita cut her husband off, saying, "Julian, don't say it, just get us some help."

Vernita contacted Ellis's mother at work and explained what happened. She ended the conversation by telling her to meet them at the hospital. Mrs. Howard was a nervous wreck. She had no idea that Robert was capable of child abuse. But he had beaten Ellis before—JW told Mrs. Howard that he had seen Ellis bruised before.

The doctor said that Ellis would be okay. He informed Mrs. Howard that her husband would face charges for the beating.

The police questioned everyone who was present when the assault occurred, and arrested Robert. Vernita encouraged Mrs. Howard to seek counseling for herself and her son. Vernita and Julian continued to give moral support to the Howards during this crisis. Robert, accompanied by his wife and son, received therapy. He voluntarily started going to church. And within months, he found another job.

Andrea stayed focused on her goals, graduated from college, and joined a prestigious architectural firm. JW was drafted to play professional basketball for the Lakers. Ellis became a beloved minister at Macedonia Baptist Church near his home town.

On April 23, 1994, Henry had been drinking heavily with some friends while watching the Lakers basketball game at his home. When the game was over, Henry escorted his guests out the front door to the driveway, shooting the breeze about the Lakers' winning streak. After waving at the last departing car, Henry went inside and grabbed another beer. He flopped down on the couch, picked up the remote control, and began flipping through the channels.

Meanwhile, Henry's nephew Lee had driven up for a visit. Knocking at the back door, he yelled, "Hey, Uncle Henry! It's Lee! Unlock this screened door, will you?"

"Lee, is that you?" Henry yelled back.

"Yep, Uncle Henry. Lee, Martha's son. Who you think it is?"

"Oh, man, I can barely see through the screen door," Henry said, as he raised his wobbly body from the couch and shuffled to the kitchen.

"Well, I see why, now! You got a brew in your hand," Lee said as he entered the room.

Lee followed Henry to the couch. As Henry was getting ready to sit down, he dropped his beer and grabbed his chest, falling to the floor.

Lee lunged to the floor, onto his knees, crouched over his uncle and shouted, "What's wrong, Uncle Henry, are you all right?"

Henry didn't respond. Lee immediately picked up the phone and dialed 911. The attendant gave Lee instructions on what to do until emergency medical personnel arrived at the scene. Though he was shaking, Lee followed instructions. He also continued to repeat, "Uncle Henry! Don't you died on me, Uncle Henry."

The ambulance soon arrived and the medical team took over. Lee telephoned his Grandma Willie Mae and told the family to meet him at the hospital because Uncle Henry had a heart attack. As the ambulance sped off, Aunt Virginia and Melissa pulled into the driveway. Lee shouted to Virginia to get back into her car, that Uncle Henry had a heart attack. Lee got into his car and followed. When they arrived at the hospital, the rest of the Turner family gradually gathered in the patients' lounge, waiting for news of Henry. Within an hour, the doctor came out and announced that Henry's condition was critical. He stated that Henry insisted on seeing his mother.

The doctor escorted Willie Mae, who was dabbing at her tears with a lacy white handkerchief, to the intensive care unit. He opened the doors for her. Seeing her son gasping for what looked like his last breaths, she quietly walked to the head of Henry's bed. She took her son's right hand in both of hers. Virginia and Melissa entered and sat in chairs at the far end of the room.

Willie Mae couldn't stop the tears, but in a firm voice, she said, "Henry, you are going to pull through this. Do you hear me, Henry?"

Henry opened his eyes. His breathless, weak voice whispered. "Ma… please forgive me."

"Forgive you for what, boy? I don't want you to try to talk. I want you to get some rest and let the doctors help you to get better. I forgave you a long time ago," Willie Mae said.

He squeezed her hands tight. "But Mom...I want you to know why... I got that dishonorable discharge from the army," Henry said. "I need to tell you.... I almost beat another soldier to death with a police weapon... while off-duty... defending his wife from spouse abuse. I lost control... started having flashbacks of when daddy beat Bro. I couldn't stop beating on him." Henry released his hard grip and closed his eyes.

Willie Mae bent down and whispered close to his ear, "Henry, don't you worry about that. The Lord has forgiven you, son. You got to forgive yourself. The Lord knows best. He doesn't hold no judgment to none of His people. That's why He died on the cross, to save us from our sins." She straightened up, looked toward Virginia and Melissa, and said in her normal voice, "Now, I don't want to hear no more. I want you to rest, Henry, and get better for mama. I love you so much."

Minutes later, Henry died peacefully.

Three years later, Bertha became ill with cancer and died on August 14, 1997. The news of Bertha's death had a tremendous impact on the community. Distant friends and relatives swamped the Turner home, expressing their condolences to the family. Four days later, funeral services were held for Bertha. Vernita and Lisa Ann each delivered a message of the memorable times they shared with their mother, gave thanks for the morals Bertha instilled upon their souls, and, on behalf of the whole family, expressed the sadness felt by this great loss. Their message brought tears of sadness, pride and joy among the congregation that had gathered in church for the funeral service.

In 1998, Martha became incapacitated and was moved into a nursing home. Dot and Bro both retired and are enjoying their families in Alabama. Susan remarried and is also living in Alabama. Irene went to college, receiving her doctorate degree in Higher Education. She is employed as Dean of the Counseling and Career Development Department at Fort Valley State University and resided with her husband, Gerald Robinson, in Perry, Georgia.

Willie Mae, at age 90, is still living in Alabama, enjoying life and sharing her experiences, wisdom, and knowledge among her children, grandchildren, and great-grandchildren.

THE END